ALSO BY NEAL POLLACK

The Neal Pollack Anthology of American Literature
Never Mind the Pollacks
Beneath the Axis of Evil
Chicago Noir (Editor)
Alternadad
Stretch

www.nealpollack.com

JEWBALL

Originally published by Neal Pollack in October 2011

Thomas & Mercer first edition 2012

Published by Thomas & Mercer
P. O. Box 400818
Las Vegas, NV 89140

ISBN-13: 9781612187235
ISBN-10: 1612187234

JEWBALL

A NOVEL

NEAL POLLACK

fTHOMAS & MERCER

FOR JEROD AND JOANNE

When der fuehrer says we is de master race
We heil heil right in der fuehrer's face...

• SPIKE JONES

PART ONE

PHILADELPHIA • 1937

THE NAZIS were watching him from the stands. Inky Lautman saw them from where he stood, at the free throw line. They hunched behind the basket in their khaki shirts, with their pinched grins, not applauding, not booing, not doing anything but silently sipping rye from little silver flasks with swastikas on the sides. What did they care about basketball? Other than transcendently stupid drunkenness, nothing mattered to them but raw hatred. When every player on the court's a Jew, the whole world loses.

The Bund, which is what the self-appointed representatives of Nazi Germany called themselves in America, had Inky worried. It was incompetent and poorly organized, not to mention constantly on the run from the Feds and extremely paranoid about spies. But there were a lot of them in Pennsylvania, and sometimes numbers meant trouble, especially when those numbers were soused to the gills.

You smug Aryan fuckers, Inky thought. *I'll work ya good.*

With ten seconds left and the South Philadelphia Hebrew Association up by four, what Inky didn't worry about was blowing the lead. His game was all about precision around the bucket. In tense times, Inky was as sharp as a well-shot arrow seeking a bull's-eye. He could sink ninety-nine out of a hundred free throws, even if the gym were on fire.

To the joy of every Jew in South Philadelphia, Inky drained the first free throw. Boys idolized and dreamed. Envy and pride stirred in the hearts of men. The end of the game would come quickly now that the league had gotten rid of that stupid rule where you jumped ball after every made basket.

At the turn of the twentieth century, basketball had been more like rugby, with no fouls, huge pileups at center court as everyone dove for the ball at once, and guys slamming one another bloody into the chicken wire that ringed the court for the spectators' safety. The ball was nearly twice the size of today's and had an inflation tube sticking out of the side, so it was hard to dribble, which was good, because the teams could only afford to replace them every two years or so. The sport advanced when they replaced the chicken wire with a metal cage. Careers would last two games, until the steel opened up a forehead or someone broke his leg in the scrum. It wasn't much fun to play, much less watch.

Dr. Naismith had invented basketball as a genteel game for good Christian boys, and he had made sure that America's colleges put it in their self-improvement programs. But those players were dull, lacking grit, style, and heart. A less polite version had been brewing in America's ghettos since before the United States entered World War I. In certain neighborhoods, it was as omnipresent as the ice wagon.

The game had its adherents among all the struggling classes— the Irish kept it gritty, and the colored players up in Harlem had style—but the Jews had been taming the game in youth centers and recreation halls in New York and Philadelphia for decades. They passed more than they punched. They established set plays and kept the fighting to a minimum. The players kept their feet on the ground when they shot; still, it began to look something like basketball.

If no one played basketball quite like the Jews, then no Jews played it quite like the South Philadelphia Hebrew Association. People respected them when they traveled around. But in Philly during the SPHAs' heyday, which lasted from the mid-twenties until the mid-forties, they were heroes, and in that respect, this night was no different from any other night.

The elaborate grand ballroom at the Broadwood Hotel had a stage, balcony, and dance floor big enough for a basketball court. Every Saturday night, they'd wheel in the hoops, lay down tape for the court boundaries, and charge sixty-five cents for men, thirty-five cents for women. The SPHAs were better than the circus. Fifteen hundred courting Jews packed together in a sweaty ballroom; it was a yenta's wet dream. The men wore jackets and trousers and sported flashy uptown hats over their yarmulkes. The women were dressed tight and shiny and classily spangled; their hemlines scraped the floor.

Tonight, like after every Saturday SPHA game, several virginities would be lost and seeds of future generations would be sown. Lips would get sucked on until they bled. Everyone was togged to the bricks and ready to stroll down Seduction Avenue. The folks in the crowd had suffered the requisite tight-quartered Shabbat with their toothless *bubbes*, whose apartments stank of boiled onion, whose stories about the Old Country were growing increasingly maudlin. Yes, yes, the Cossacks killed your cows and burned your synagogue. Your pain is immense. Thank you for sharing. But now it's Saturday night.

These grandchildren victims of post-shtetl nostalgia needed to cut loose in so many ways. First, basketball, to give them the giddy feeling of belonging to something bigger and sweatier than themselves, and then, with the team victorious, a big band concert, a high-end Hebrew tribal mating dance where the women would share in the glee of victory. The time for celebration had arrived.

Much to their disappointment, Inky called time-out.

By the time he reached the bench, he could see that he'd pissed off Gottlieb. The coach's head looked like a tomato about to burst out of its skin. He'd half undone his bow tie. What hair he had left was stuck to his head with furious sweat. Inky prepared for the onslaught.

"Hey, Lautman! Let me ask you something."

"Yes, Eddie?"

"Did the Lord Our God appear to you after you ate challah last night? Did he order you, via divine prophecy, to call time-out at the end of a game that your team had already won? Because that's the only possible excuse I'm going to accept here, you fucknut."

"No, Eddie," Inky said.

"Maybe you should remember who the coach is here. Huh? Huh? I draw up the plays. I make the substitutions. Oh, and to add to the absolute superiority I hold over your tiny point guard ass in every way, I also pay your salary, book your tours, and get every sports-loving hack with a typewriter in town to write about you like you crap diamonds for breakfast. So maybe, just maybe, you might want to fucking consult me before you decide to call time-out! And furthermore—"

"Bund," Inky said. "Ten o'clock."

He pointed to where the Nazis had been sitting. They were getting up and moving to strategic locations near courtside. Gottlieb gave a low moan. This had become a common problem. When the SPHAs had started rolling in the Jazz Age, it had been all Jews buying tickets, with the occasional cluster of Negro or

Italian fans. But every year since the rise of Hitler, the proportion of serious Jew-haters in the stands had grown. Some games it got close to fifty-fifty, and the haters didn't have their dates along to encourage them to pull their punches.

"Fucking Bund," he said. "At least once a month…"

Gottlieb motioned for the team to gather round. He ran a rag over his chalkboard and handed it to Inky.

"You got any ideas, Lautman?" he said.

"One or two," Inky said.

Inky quickly sketched out a line of defense, with a player standing sentry at each possible point of entry onto the court. They'd square off the perimeter, and if the Nazis decided to cluster, they could close ranks quickly.

"Fitch," Inky said, "I've got something special for you."

"Let me guess," Gil Fitch said, "you want me to get the band together."

This was what everyone always wanted Fitch to do. Fitch had been playing the alto saxophone since he was eleven years old. In 1936, he decided that being a basketball player in a semi-pro Jewish league wouldn't pay the bills forever and decided to start a band. Gottlieb hired him to play concerts after the games on Saturday night. It would boost ticket sales and get gals into the stands. They had a fifteen-year-old girl singer named Kitty Kallen. Fitchy had heard her on the Kiddy Hour on WCAU and decided she had to front his orchestra. He agreed to drive her home after every gig, and seeing as how Kitty wasn't pregnant yet, her mother continued to trust him.

"Go to the locker and get your sax," Inky said.

"I usually shower first," said Fitch.

"No time tonight," Inky said. "Play in your uniform. Look sweaty. Strike up at the buzzer. It'll sow confusion."

Fitch stood up.

Inky slapped him on the butt. "Hustle," he said.

Over on the bench, handsome Cy Kaselman, known as "Sun-dodger" for his amazing ability to fall asleep during any situation, no matter how stressful or noisy, was nodding off.

"Hey, Sundodger," said Inky.

Kaselman snorted awake.

"Sleeping all day not good enough for you?"

"Guy can never get enough sleep," Kaselman said.

"I need an ambassador to Cleveland. Get over there."

"What do you want me to tell them?" Cy asked.

"That we're about to get attacked."

"Seriously?"

Inky gestured around the arena.

"Open your eyes, Sundodger," he said. "It's 1937 and the Bund is everywhere."

Kaselman stood up and yawned.

"Noisy bastards," he said, and sauntered over to Cleveland's bench to enlist help. Once the games ended, team loyalties gave way to ancient tribal ties. The Rosenblums had plenty of experience brawling with Ohio bigots, who were just the same as Pennsylvania bigots, only with flatter accents.

The time-out ended, but Inky hadn't finished sketching his battle plan. When the refs came over and ordered the SPHAs back on the court, he called another time-out. Now boos cascaded, as Inky's scheming began to forestall several hundred Saturday-night boners. According to one angry nearby fan, the SPHAs were small-dicked sheep fuckers who didn't deserve his hard-earned money. Usually guys who talked like that came to the game accompanied by a prostitute.

Inky ignored the crowd. They would have to sacrifice their petty desires to the greater good. Instead, he looked down the end of the bench toward Shostack. Every squad needed a Shostack, a plodding behemoth rebounder, to counter the opposition's plodding behemoth rebounder. They didn't play often in these games, because it was all about speed, not power. King Kong can't swat flies. But in times of crisis, it helped to have a really big brisket on your side.

Shostack was studying sheet music. He had a violin audition with the symphony in a couple of days. Inky walked over.

"Charlie."

Shostack looked up, surprised.

"Me?" he said.

"I need you to set a pick," Inky said.

"Now?" he said. "This is a really complicated concerto."

"The Bund don't give a fuck about your violin, Shostack."

"I hate the Bund."

"And the Bund hates you. So I need you to throw picks when I call them out."

"Glad to know I come in handy for something."

"Couldn't live without you, sweetie."

"You are a user of men, Inky."

"Only when I need them," Inky said.

The SPHAs went back onto the court and lined up in battle formation. Inky bricked the shot. The Rosenblums got the rebound, driving down undefended for a layup at the buzzer. *Mark these guys for a thirty-point loss next time,* Inky thought. But he had bigger problems than a little Cleveland showboating. The Bund had managed to pool behind the beer stand, relatively undefended territory, and they were pouring onto the court toward him, fists raised. They'd already broken through his defenses. Maybe someday Gottlieb would realize Inky didn't have any idea how to sketch a fight plan.

"Shostack!" Inky called out. "Set a pick!"

Shostack slid into place and sent a meaty elbow straight into the face of the first arrival. Inky slid under the blow of the second guy, sending him sprawling to the pine with a vicious leg sweep. He hopped on the guy's bloated Bund belly, jammed a knee into his gut, grabbed his greasy blond hair, and slammed his head to the floor.

Fitch's orchestra, some still in their undershirts, had bumbled out of the locker room and hurried into a Duke Ellington number. The crowd whooped like this was some sort of ultra-violent postgame celebration. A thin line separates a sports fan's passion from actual bloodlust.

By this time the players had caught up to the Bund flood. They leaped over one another's backs to get in their punches. Inky could see that they were clustered too tightly, but he hadn't had time to form platoons. His half-baked correctional instructions weren't going to get heard in the mess. He just kept calling out picks and hoping for the best.

Then someone hit Harry Litwack in the head with a Coke bottle and it all went to hell. You could beat up Jews with impunity across large swaths of Philadelphia, but if you tried to draw Litwack blood, you were asking for problems. Even the goyim worshipped Litwack. He was the golden god of the SPHAs, their best player, the one they could trot out onto the podium at city hall ceremonies. Inky thought Litwack was a self-righteous attention hog, and he hated being on his team come playoff time. The tougher things got, the easier Litwack took them, and he behaved impeccably in all circumstances. He never got a technical foul, always got the newspaper headlines, and he'd be hailed as a civic institution for decades to come.

The bottle cracked Litwack at center court. Litwack staggered back into the Nazi, who swung again, grazing Harry's left temple. Litwack put his hand to the top of his head. He fell to his knees. His opponent moved in for the kill. But he would never get there. The pig pile was on.

All the players had seen the attack. They left whomever they were hammering with their fists and ran toward the guy who'd gone after Litwack. The crowd had seen it too. Guys who thought their ladies liked it rough rushed down the aisle. At most, there were thirty Bundsmen on the court, giving them a two-to-one advantage over the players. But they'd incited the mob, and the ballroom really started to shake.

When they realized that they were outnumbered, the Bundsmen began to scatter. Then the doors to the ballroom burst open, revealing Bund reinforcements, half of them off-duty cops who'd been waiting outside. They charged in, yelling nonsense. Hitler's wife's dogs had more discipline than these guys. Still, thanks to this fresh order of beef, the fight drew even again. Fitch ordered the band to play faster and louder.

People grabbed whatever they could, mostly chairs. The court was getting slick now with sweat and a little blood, and there was slipping. Hundreds of fans poured toward the exit, almost colliding with the blue shirts as a phalanx of cops charged toward the court. Inky saw a Bundsman go for his shoe, with a flash of silver. Inky was a sometime biter. He'd grown up in South Philly and he knew how to play dirty. He was on the guy, teeth buried in his shoulder like a rottweiler, before he could do any damage with the knife.

The police had batons drawn now. They formed a tight circle around Litwack, which is what Inky had wanted to pull off with the players in the first place. Two of the cops put Harry on a stretcher and carried him away. Litwack, always looking for the main PR chance, sat up, smiled, and waved a bloody hand at the crowd.

"Doin' okay, chief!" he said.

The crowd roared in approval. Meanwhile, the cops had grabbed Inky, and Shostack, and Gottlieb.

"What the hell are you doing?" Inky said. "The Bund started it."

"We ain't arresting you," said a cop. "We're escorting you to a safe location."

"Escort THE BUND!" Inky shouted.

Gottlieb motioned for him to be quiet.

"Inky, their chief is *in* the Bund," he said. "Half the guys who attacked us are too. We're lucky to still have our kneecaps." Gottlieb shook his head and sighed. "Fucking Bund."

Meanwhile, Shostack was shaking his right hand.

"This is pretty sore," he said. "I've got an audition Monday."

"Stick it in the icebox, big man," Inky said.

"I wish you'd stick your *head* in the icebox," said Shostack.

"Hey! This ain't my fault!"

"You shoulda had Litwack draw up the plan," Shostack said. "*That* guy knows how to organize a defense."

Some thanks Inky got for trying to be a hero to his people. Little did they understand. As he sat in the back of the police wagon, trying to guess how big the welts would grow, he dreamed of a golden tomorrow. All he wanted was to play basketball, and really, he didn't even want to do that. He was just looking for a place where other people didn't beat up Jews and where Jews didn't beat up other people. Was that so much for a guy to ask?

As soon as I find that place, he thought, *I'm going to move there, or at least visit for a little while during the summer. You know, to try it out.*

· t w o ·

MOST OF the players who shot for the SPHAs came from burgher backgrounds. Their parents or grandparents had made all the necessary immigrant sacrifices, and all paths pointed upward. The players had college degrees and off-season careers. Some of them had acquired a wife or a kid, or both. Litwack would have the whole package until the day he died, a day that would create headlines up and down the length of the Jersey Shore.

Inky's cards told a different tale.

While the rest of the country had appeared to float on a Jazz Age bubble during a return to normalcy, Inky lived with his parents in a drafty two-bedroom apartment in a crappy sand-mortared building somewhere east of Broad and south of hell. His father had been a machinist with a fondness for corn liquor, which was all he'd been able to obtain, much less afford, during the less-than-halcyon Prohibition days of Inky's boyhood. The man had reproduced late and had given up even before Inky was born.

He'd spent his Saturdays staring out the greasy back window, trying to get a glimpse of some kind of water over the smokestacks and warehouses, whistling a half-forgotten love ballad through his yellowed teeth, smelling like rot and chemicals.

One fine day in 1925, just after Inky had gotten home from school, a man he'd never seen before came to the door. The man's overalls were splattered with blood, his eyes wide and vague, like people's eyes get when they've just witnessed some sort of unimaginable horror. There'd been an accident at the factory. Inky's father slipped on the assembly line and the circular saw had ripped through his arm just below the shoulder.

Inky stood there as this stranger told him the gruesome details of his father's death. He wasn't the type to cry at this kind of news; he'd numbed young. His father's blood had pumped from a severed artery like water from a hydrant, and he'd died within two minutes. They'd found a fifth in his uniform pocket and were going to blame the accident on that. And they'd probably be right to do so, Inky thought sadly.

Inky's mother came to the door, asked what was happening, and the shell-shocked coworker repeated the entire sorry tale. Now this woman who had been making Inky's father sleep on the sofa for half a decade began ululating with the volume of an entire Polish village. Now she mourned. How would she survive? What about her children? What about her *babies*? But some strange worm of senility had already begun eating away at Ma's brain, and Inky knew that, in an hour, she'd be on her bed, silently humming while gazing at a photo of herself when she was very young and thought that she was very beautiful. Things hadn't been right in that house for quite some time. It already swam in dust and filth, and now she'd found the excuse she wanted to let it go for good.

They publicly mourned at a neighbor's house a few days later. Inky got glad-handed, like a convention-going Shriner, by a parade of insincere strangers in ill-fitting suits, most of whom had come to gawk at the grief-stricken widow and mooch off the buffet. Then, as always, untimely death made for good snacking. Young Inky picked at a half-warm piece of kugel and looked for a way out.

A hulking *alter kocker* approached. Inky had seen him before at his father's poker nights, which had always ended with the old man out double-digit bucks and asleep under the dining room table, an empty bottle carelessly tucked under his arm like a football about to be fumbled. The old fart took Inky's hand. His breath smelled like a bison's.

"A tragedy," the beast said in a marbly baritone. "A terrible tragedy."

Inky didn't know how to respond to that. He knew tragedy full well. But he didn't know what the word meant.

The guy leaned in close. "Today you are a man," he said.

What a load.

For the first time in his life, which admittedly hadn't been that long, Inky felt *clarity*. He saw through everything, the falseness, the pretension, the standing death that awaited him if he bought in for five seconds what was being offered up in that room, the burden of five thousand years of tradition being used as a smoke screen to mask that he was a nothing, sired by a nothing, doomed to nothingness. But he did have something that no one else in the room could boast: a fertile combination of youth, anger, and speed. Those traits would serve him well for many years.

Inky feinted left and slipped away from the man's grip. He dodged through the room, past the low-renters, the classless sycophants of his classless life, and he left less impression than a breeze. His mother, sitting in the corner simultaneously bemoaning her lousy fortune and lost in a haze of boardwalk memories, didn't notice a thing. Inky launched himself down the stoop into the dead air, running past the ice trucks and the candy stores, just another ghetto kid sprinting through the ghetto trying to escape his ghetto destiny, running away from everything, from his luck-less birth and his lousy education and his fraying shirt cuffs, try-ing to forget who he was and trying to find another way of being.

Along came basketball.

Every sooty phone pole in Jewish Philadelphia had a peach basket on it. Every alleyway was filled with the *thwang* of leather on asphalt or, in the less developed neighborhoods, the mellower sounds of leather on dirt. And every boy worth his bar mitzvah legacy wanted to play. On that day, the day when the world put his father's memory to rest for good, Louis "Inky" Lautman joined their number.

He came upon an alley. There, five boys (a couple around his age, the others older, and all taller than he was) were taking turns, and taking aim, at the basket. But they clearly seemed bored. Inky stopped and watched. He was many blocks from home. These boys wouldn't know him from Greenbaum.

The ball got away and rolled to Inky's feet. Inky stared at it as though it had just fallen from the sky.

"Hey, shorty!" one of the boys shouted.

"Me?" Inky said.

"You gonna give us our ball?"

"Sure," Inky said.

Inky picked up the ball. It felt smooth and worn, totally natu-ral in his hands, like he was putting on his best pair of overalls.

"Throw it, you ass!"

Inky drew back the ball to his chest, crooked his elbows, and shot a decent-looking bounce pass down the alley. The boys looked impressed. Inky had no idea why.

"You play?" asked another boy.

"No," Inky said.

"You want to? We need a sixth."

"Okay."

"Why you wearing a tie?"

"My pop died."

"That's too bad."

"Yeah."

Inky stood there, looking into the alley. They threw him the ball. He didn't know what to do.

"Bounce it," said the kid.

Inky did.

"Again."

Inky loosened his tie and dribbled in. Within a minute, the tie was off and lying on a trash can lid. A minute after that, Inky was in his shirtsleeves. He played three-on-three, not very well. But the guys liked having him in the mix. He picked up the rules easily and he was fast enough. Inky had the instinct, even then, to pass the ball, to scrap, to dive to the ground, to put his kneecap where it shouldn't go. His team won the first game, and then they switched players. Inky got cocky. He started shooting a lot. But he had no technique and no accuracy. This time, his team lost. The seeds of a basketball lesson had been planted.

They played until the streetlamps came on, five hours or more, and then a little longer, until the kids' moms came out of nowhere and dragged them by their ears toward home. But no one showed to drag Inky home. No one ever would. The kids left the ball behind and Inky shot it until the moon shone over the rooftops, and then he shot a couple hours more.

From then on, Inky, untethered from adult supervision, spent his voluminous free time in every alley and on any playground he could find. He worked the leather. When he needed a ball, he stole one. When he couldn't find one to steal, he took money from his mother and bought one. He practiced shooting until his fingernails bled, and he dribbled until blisters bloomed on the heels of his hands. Often, he played pretty well. Even when he didn't play well, he played hard. He went from last picked to the middle of the pack. By the time a year had passed, they knew him in the alleys and were letting him act as captain of his own team.

He was never the fastest or the strongest or the best shooter; no one would ever say that Inky Lautman had the total package. He was too short and a little squat. But he didn't stop, he couldn't stop, it never even occurred to him, and by the end of any game, everyone knew that Inky was the court boss. *Let the other players score*, Inky said to himself. At the end of the day, he'd hold the keys.

Inky Lautman: born to run the point.

A reputation developed as Inky made the alley rounds. He got invited to play on actual courts. Compared with those tight spaces he'd started in, with their barely tolerable stench of rotting fish heads and discarded apple cores, playing on a hardwood floor and shooting at hoops with actual backboards seemed easy. He felt like a hobo who'd somehow inherited a mansion. Inky glided up and down the court with pure focus, seeing every opportunity and grabbing as many as he could. Any guy who happened to land on Inky's team knew that there'd be at least a chance to win that day.

High school came early at age thirteen, not because Inky had done anything of interest in the classroom, but because the team needed a point guard. The coach paid off the necessary school authorities, and Inky was in. So once again, he found himself just about the smallest guy on the court, and once again, his play dominated because no one hustled harder. The games had official clocks and official scorers and actual fans, including more than one girl who showed Inky a tantalizing flash of knee. With the fans came the boosters and the reporters, and for the first time, the Lautman name meant something in Philadelphia other than a drunk tank asterisk in the police blotter. By the middle of Inky's sophomore year, the gym was full for every game. A promoter wrote a song about him. "Hey, hey, Inky / The fastest Jew in school" went the lyrics. No one ever claimed it was a good song, and it left a slim mark on the culture of the town.

One night, after a typical game where Inky had scored twenty-two points with twenty-two assists, seven rebounds, nine steals, four fouls, and one technical foul for a knee to another player's groin, his eyes wandered up to the bleachers, where a flame-eyed gal was staring at him and running her tongue around her lips. Inky thought he might dip his toe. On his way up the stairs, destiny intercepted him, in the form of an overweight cigar chomper in his midthirties who was unimaginably sweaty all over even though it was barely March. Inky tried his usual dodge, but the guy didn't bite. No mere sophomore was going to get past that wall.

"Inky Lautman?" the guy said, extending his hand.

"Yeah?" Inky said, not extending his.

"Eddie Gottlieb," the man said.

"So?"

"So I own the SPHAs."

"That's good for you."

"I haven't seen you around the Hebrew Association much lately. Or ever."

"I don't go in for the religion."

"I don't either. We've got the best courts in town."

"I do okay without the best courts."

"You do more than okay, kid. You've got the best basketball sense of anyone I've seen in twenty years."

"Yeah?"

"Yeah."

"Well, fuck you, Gottlieb. I got a date."

Gottlieb looked up at Inky's date.

"That broad?"

"Yeah."

"You can't afford her."

"Why not?"

"Because she's a hooker."

"And how do you know that?"

"Believe me," Gottlieb said. "I run a basketball team. I know a hooker in the stands when I see one."

"Yeah, well, maybe I can get something for free."

"That kind of defeats her purpose," Gottlieb said. "The more you think of yourself, the more she'll charge you. But I guess you need to learn these things on your own."

Inky brushed past.

"Hey, Lautman?" Gottlieb said.

"What?" Inky said.

"What do you say I come by your house sometime and meet your parents?"

"Ain't much to meet. My pop's dead and my ma might as well be."

"Sorry to hear that."

"It's a fact, that's all."

"Anyway, I've got a business proposition."

"What the hell does that mean?"

"It means you wanna play ball for the SPHAs, you dumb heeb?"

"Does it mean I have to play with you?"

"No, but it means you have to play *for* me."

"Maybe not, then," Inky said.

Inky gave Gottlieb his address anyway. Gottlieb looked surprised. He said that with an address like that, he'd better stop by before sundown, to increase his odds of ending his day alive. Inky told Gottlieb to go sit on a pole. They'd quickly figured out how to talk to each other.

Gottlieb showed up the next afternoon. Inky answered the door. When he opened it, dust swirled. The apartment smelled old.

"Guess you really need a point guard," Inky said.

"I might," Gottlieb said. "Guess you really need a maid."

"It's her week off," Inky said. "Make it quick. I got practice in half an hour."

"Is your mother at home?"

Inky shouted toward the back of the house. "MA! We got company!"

Ma Lautman staggered out of the back, where she'd been boiling onions even though she didn't plan to eat them. By now, she had the look and demeanor of a stygian witch, complete with rags. She appraised Gottlieb up and down.

"Why are you so fat?" she asked.

"Because I like to eat," Gottlieb said.

"Ma," Inky said, "this is Mr. Gottlieb. He wants me to play basketball for the SPHAs."

"What are SPHAs?"

"The South Philadelphia Hebrew All-Stars, Mrs. Lautman," Gottlieb said. "It's a professional basketball team."

"They're the best team there is," Inky said.

Gottlieb looked surprised. This was the first sign of enthusiasm he'd seen Inky show about anything. No fifteen-year-old should have been able to keep his cool at such a prospect. Maybe the kid was normal after all.

"Professional basketball," Mrs. Lautman said. "Does that mean you get paid?"

"I pay my boys well," Gottlieb said. "Meals and travel too."

Ma Lautman pondered this for a few seconds. She turned to her son.

"Inky," she said, "is this what you want to do?"

"I don't know," he said.

She turned to Gottlieb.

"Is he any good?"

"Oh, he's very good," Gottlieb said.

"Damn right I'm good," said Inky.

"But he can get better."

"No thanks to you."

"You should do it, son," Ma said.

"Okay, Ma," Inky said.

Gottlieb pulled out Inky's contract. The timing was good for Inky, because six months later, people would be jumping out of Manhattan skyscrapers. At such times, it was good to have steady work.

"I need you both to sign," he said. "Inky's underage."

"Sign what?" Ma Lautman said.

"Inky's contract," said Gottlieb.

"Contract for what?"

"For playing basketball."

"Inky doesn't play basketball," said Ma. "He's just a baby."

Inky moaned with frustration. Gottlieb felt less like a basketball coach and more like a charity worker. But at least he had himself a point guard.

Within a month, Inky was playing professional basketball. By the following month, he had his pick of girls from the stands. He didn't have to pay for any of them, though some of them were fairly nice girls and wanted dinner first. But girls weren't the only ones watching Inky. Everyone paid attention to the show runner, the tough, no-bullshit guy at the center of the action. Inky didn't care. His early years had given him a hard, mercenary approach to life, and it showed on the court.

The Depression hit. Fascism in Europe followed. Inky had a job and didn't care for politics. He figured everyone was just looking for a cut of whatever action they could generate. So he just kept playing basketball. This made Inky the perfect mark for a certain type.

One night in the winter of 1935, a man came up to Inky after a game. He had pale cheeks, a thin mustache, and little round spectacles. The games had been attracting all kinds of customers.

"Mr. Lautman?" the guy said.

"Yeah?" said Inky.

"My name is Gerhard Wilhelm Kunze. I represent an organization."

"So?"

"I enjoyed your game tonight."

"What's that to me?" Inky said.

"Maybe a lot."

"Get to the point," Inky said, pointing at a hot number powdering her nose in the stands. "I got a date."

"Okay, I will."

"Not quick enough."

"How'd you like to make a little extra money?"

Now Inky was listening.

three

A SUN the color of rancid butter wrenched itself over the rim of the Delaware. Even before the newsboys left home with their sacks of lies, the air smelled like a barge. It was the kind of morning that would have heralded a cholera epidemic during the glorious founding of the republic in the historic city of Philadelphia.

After spending an achy, sleepless night in a downtown holding cell, where Shostack had snored on his shoulder and Gottlieb had farted like an elderly dog, Inky got off the day's first Girard trolley feeling like a hair floating in a bowl of lukewarm soup. Grim thoughts swarmed around his brain like the day's mosquitoes that would soon float up from the sewers.

He turned the corner at the Bucket. A shaggy-haired Pole who'd somehow happened into the city's first post-Prohibition distillery license had opened the place with his sister four years prior. They rented Inky the room overhead and, at least once a week, let him "tie up the dog" at the bar. Inky paid them back by sometimes beating up deadbeats who wouldn't pay their tabs or tried playing grab ass with the sister more than once.

A table and two chairs, a cot, a teakettle and a gas stove, a punching bag, and a few basketball-related newspaper clippings on the wall so Inky could remember that he existed when he woke up in the morning—it wasn't much of a room, and it always smelled like rubbing alcohol. But it was free. By the time someone made it up to his room, he'd already impressed them. Inky only hosted interested parties.

His one indulgence was a new GE refrigerator, which he'd leased on credit from Sears. They gave easy terms to local stars. They sold it to him for $230, a small fortune. Inky had the money and few other expenses. Inside, he kept steaks that he picked out at the kosher slaughterhouse in Mount Airy.

Inky grabbed a sirloin, wrenched down onto his cot, and put the steak over his throbbing right eye, which was sprouting a disturbing goose egg. An unshaded lightbulb swung tenuously overhead. He lit a Viceroy. The last twelve hours had mostly been bullshit, he determined. He didn't like to think much more deeply than that; he saved the majority of his intelligence for ball distribution.

The cigarette having done its job with a cellulose-acetate kicker, Inky extinguished it into a beer bottle and, at last, fell into a bitterly exhausted sleep. By the time he saw consciousness again, the sun had moved on to baking West Philly and Lower Merion. But it was still a swamp outside. He'd sweated through the sheet, his undershirt, everything. Small puddles had gathered at the head of his cot. His mouth felt woolly and his eyes leaden. He got up, put his head under the faucet for what seemed like about fifteen minutes, and that was when the Bund busted down his door.

Inky looked up from the sink, a towel that he'd swiped from the SPHAs' equipment manager around his neck. In his doorway stood two pieces of kraut flesh, men the color, texture, and with the intelligence of bratwurst. They wore short-sleeved white shirts and khaki slacks. Everything appeared to be soaked, as though they'd walked through a swollen river to get here. They were heaving like a couple of animals. Ernst and Helmut, fat brothers from Germantown. Inky knew them. Sometimes he worked with them.

When Inky wasn't playing basketball, he stayed down low, on the fringes, doing things for money that the new class of good Jewish boys didn't, and he didn't tell anyone about his side work. It had been almost three years since he'd started muscling for the Bund. Its leaders paid him well, sometimes very well, to do out-of-state shakedown work; they funded their rallies largely through bookmaking operations. Inky mostly got sent to rough up the black clientele.

When he'd first signed on, Inky had told the Bund that he "didn't give a fuck about being Jewish." He harbored a secret ethnic resentment toward himself, a kind of extreme, if repressed, self-hatred. Whence it sprang, he didn't know, and because he didn't know, he didn't care. But it sat in his gut, deep and strong. The Bund leaders latched onto this particular psychological quality right off. Combined with Inky's almost complete lack of higher formal education, it left him in a state of almost unparalleled political apathy. It also made him a good hire.

The brothers had busted the latch and one of the hinges.

"I answer to knocks," Inky said.

"Kunze wants to see you," Ernst said.

"Fuck Kunze."

"Not what we wanted to hear you say."

"What'd you expect, after the way you guys acted last night?"

"That's what you get for showing your hairy monkey legs in public," said Helmut. "You Jews are apes."

The Germans laughed. They sounded phlegmy, like they had mustard spouting out of their noses. Inky whipped his wet towel at them, and they flinched.

"At least I've got legs to show," said Inky. "All you got are meat tubes with feet."

They ignored the insult.

"There's a job for you," Helmut said.

"I don't work for the Bund no more," said Inky.

"Kunze says you do."

"No. Not even sometimes."

"This job is different. It's Jew related."

"Then I'm definitely not doing it."

Inky picked up his pack of Viceroys, slid one out, and lit it with his Zippo, another indulgence that he'd recently purchased.

"Athletes shouldn't smoke," Ernst said.

"I'm only an athlete when I'm bein' athletic," Inky said.

The Germans began to shuffle impatiently.

"You comin' or what, Inky?"

"I got people to see for dinner."

"You can see them after you see Kunze."

"The next time I want to see Kunze is when we bunk together in hell."

Ernst pulled a gun.

"Come with us now," he said.

"You wouldn't shoot a Jew, would you?" Inky said.

"I wouldn't *not* shoot a Jew…"

Inky gathered the German was serious. He picked up a chair and whipped it across the room. The chair knocked the German's hand downward. The gun fired. A bullet went through Ernst's shoe and struck flesh, making the sound that a pumpkin makes when you drop it from the roof.

"*Scheisse!*" the German shouted. He went down on a knee. Blood was seeping out of his shoe. He'd probably need orthotics moving forward.

Meanwhile, Helmut, in a moment of practical thinking, had drawn his own gun. Inky didn't feel like further maneuvering. It must have been a serious situation if *both* these bonehead henchmen were pulling lead.

"This ain't no scrimmage, Inky," he said.

"All right, all right," Inky said, "I'll go see Kunze. Just let me put on some fucking pants."

Ernst sat on the floor, moaning like a toddler who'd lost his toy horsey. Inky reached under his bed, where he kept a box of torn cloth for just such occasions. He tossed a thick strip to the German.

"You know how to make a tourniquet?" he asked.

The German whimpered. Inky felt bad for him. Then again, he hadn't *forced* fatty to draw his gat.

"You can stop the bleeding with that," Inky said. "We'll drop you off at Kensington Memorial on the way. Right, Helmut?"

"What?" Helmut said.

"Useless," said Inky. "Tell them you were cleaning the gun when it went off. So, Helmut, you gonna let me drive?"

"No," Helmut said.

"Just thought I'd ask. Now let's get out of here before your brother bleeds to death on my floor."

four

THE HEADQUARTERS of fascism in Philadelphia was a third-floor walk-up apartment, accessible only via the back stairs of a print shop and bookstore at 3718 North Fifth Street, a short walk from the geographic center of Bund activity at Sixth and Erie. The print shop's proprietor, an exiled Estonian aristocrat, czarist sympathizer, and former shipping company executive named Count Paul von Lilienfeld-Toal, specialized in collecting cheap copies of *Mein Kampf* and the works of Julius Streicher as well as such fine newspapers as *Das Schwarze Korps* and the *American Gentile*, and the well-loved *Philadelphia Deutscher Weckruf und Beobachter*, which featured a swastika on its masthead. Count von Lilienfeld-Toal also enjoyed writing pamphlets about how the Jewish domination of the American food-processing industry would cause a nationwide plague. This, he wrote, would make "the conquest of America easier for certain Oriental interests who will play with the Soviet regime." The Bund got its space rent free.

Inky walked up the stairs, Helmut poking him from behind with his useless gun. Opening the door to the office, Inky beheld the decidedly non-*Götterdämmerung* sight of the count playing chess with Gerhard Wilhelm Kunze, the Bund's national public relations director and deputy führer, second only to Fritz Julius Kuhn, confidant of Hitler and head of the party.

They called Kunze the "Goebbels of the Bund," partly because he had such a big mouth. He believed in the elimination of international Jewry and maintaining a white man's United States, which could be achieved by the passing of "race legislation." Jews, he once said in a speech, were atheists and Marxists, "the small, ever-homeless minority which alone has anything to gain by tearing nations asunder and by pitting them against themselves and each other." Hitler he described as "the greatest man since the time of Christ." Kunze was a real peach.

"Ah," Kunze said, "our errand boy. Can we offer you some coffee?"

"Nah," Inky said. "Your coffee has too much flavor."

"Suit yourself."

"What do you want, Kunze?"

"You've been a reliable cog for the Bund, Inky," Kunze said. "Against the best interests of your race."

Inky spat on the floor.

"Only because you pay good," he said.

"As always," Kunze said, "the Jew parasite is trying to suck at the teat of the Aryan race, who created these great United States."

"I just upped my rates," Inky said.

"Wise. Especially because the money we lent to your boss Gottlieb is coming due."

"Gottlieb wouldn't borrow money from you clowns."

"Obviously not, but he *would* borrow money from the Irish mob. Who, in turn, would sell us the loan, as long as we paid a little extra."

"How much does he owe?" Inky said.

"Eight grand."

Inky gave a low whistle.

"He ain't gonna be able to pay that back right away," Inky said. "And I ain't gonna make him."

"He doesn't have to pay it back."

"Makes sense."

"We know how Jews hate to part with their money," said Kunze. "So we have another option."

Kunze then detailed a plan, crafted among the highest-ranking members of the North American Bund to humble the arrogant Jews by vanquishing their hard-court heroes. The Bund had assembled a basketball team of Teutonic giants, which he called the Aryan All-Stars. They were training, at this very moment, in Minneapolis. The Bund proposed an exhibition contest between them and the Jewish championship team, which was bound to be the SPHAs. Rather than repaying his chit, Gottlieb just needed to take his team to Minnesota and ensure that it went down to overwhelming defeat.

"This will prove to the American sports fan," Kunze said, "the final and ultimate superiority of the Aryan race over lesser Continental interlopers. It is our plan."

"That's just crazy," Inky said.

Kunze raised an eyebrow.

"Is it, now?" he said. "Or is it a product of a higher intelligence?"

"Nope, crazy," Inky said. "We like to lose even less than we like to part with our money."

"Which would you prefer? A humiliating loss or to have the Bund own and subsequently disband your team?"

"Not for me to decide."

"We need you to talk to Gottlieb."

"What if he says no?"

"If he says no, we want you to torch his office. Make it look on purpose so he can't collect."

"What if I don't want to torch his office?"

"Then we know where you live."

"Ask Helmut if that matters. I defend my territory well."

"We'll give you three hundred dollars."

They had found Inky's weak spot. That would more than pay off his icebox.

"I'll talk to Gottlieb," he said.

On his way out the door, Inky flipped the chessboard. Lukewarm coffee went everywhere.

"Jew to queen eight," he said.

· f i v e ·

EDDIE GOTTLIEB sat in his office above Passon's Sporting Goods near Fifth and Market, nursing a tall glass of cold water with double Alka-Seltzer. He was looking at the books. They didn't look great. Next to him, a tubby young guy in a cheap suit nervously turned the ledger pages. They had the windows open and a plus-sized Westinghouse going in the corner, but they were both sweating enough to warp the floorboards.

"The money is not flowing my way, Zink," Gottlieb said.

"Yes, Eddie," said the young guy.

"I don't like it when that happens."

"No, Eddie."

The young guy gulped nervously. This was Dave Zinkoff, the SPHAs' public-address announcer. He also handled publicity and promotions. If times were rough, and even if they weren't, Gottlieb was always threatening to fire him.

The pattern had been set early. When Zinkoff applied to be the SPHAs' public-address announcer, he went to the offices at Fifth and Market.

"Stand over there and say forty words," Eddie had said to him.

So he did that, and then Gottlieb said to him, "Now face the wall and say forty words."

He did that too, and then he got the job, having met Gottlieb's very odd criteria. Soon Zinkoff brought innovations to the promotional end. Before every SPHAs game, he'd hand out a free salami from his father's delicatessen at Fortieth and Girard. He also instituted the "lucky number," included inside someone's program at every home game, which guaranteed the winner a suit, valued at $19.95, from Sam Gerson's store at Sixth and Bainbridge. In addition, he drove the team on road trips when Gottlieb was drunk.

Not unjustifiably, one day Zinkoff asked for a raise. He was making five bucks a week. He wanted six.

"Why?" Gottlieb said.

"Because I'm doing a good job. People are coming to hear me announce."

"Let's see."

"See what?"

"See how you like handing out programs instead."

So Gottlieb fired Zinkoff, gave him a job in the stands, and hired a new announcer. After two weeks, Zinkoff couldn't take the humiliation anymore. He walked down to the bench before a game one night.

"Eddie, I want my old job back," he said.

Gottlieb looked around. Every seat was full.

"It doesn't look like we lost any customers," Gottlieb said.

"Just give me my job back, Eddie. Okay?"

Eddie respected men who talked to him like that. He shouted over to the scorer's table. He slapped a five and a one into Zinkoff's hand.

"Figured you might want an advance on this week's pay," he said.

Ever since, Zinkoff had been his lackey. He pretty much did whatever Gottlieb wanted. True to form, he was fanning Gottlieb with a newspaper when Inky walked in.

"Ah, my floor captain," Gottlieb said. "How can I be of service?"

"Eddie, I got bad news."

"Of course you do," Gottlieb said.

"I just paid a little visit to the Bund," Inky said. "It wasn't my choice. They came to get me."

"To the *what*?" Eddie said.

"The Bund."

"Why the *fuck* would you do that?"

Inky explained enough to let Gottlieb know that he'd accidentally borrowed a lot of money from the burgeoning American branch of Adolf Hitler's empire. Gottlieb looked as though thrombosis were setting in. He stood and waved his hands.

"Those tickets were from the micks!" Gottlieb said. "And they were a sure thing!"

"Hold on a second…" Zinkoff said. "You risked the team's future on Irish sweepstakes tickets?"

Gottlieb hissed at him like an angry cat.

"I wasn't going to pay them back!" Gottlieb said. "I had an in."

"The sweepstakes, Eddie?" Zinkoff said. "Really? Ain't that illegal?"

"We were in debt. Creditors were threatening to fold up the chairs. They sold me forty thousand tickets and said I was guaranteed a share of the prize."

"Come on, Eddie. Borrowing money to pay for Irish sweep-stakes tickets? You know that's a scam. Couldn't you just have gotten a loan from your brother-in-law or something?"

"Hey, fucknut, you want me to pay your salary? I have over-head here!"

Inky stood there with his arms crossed. Gottlieb gave a little sigh, more like a moan. He pulled a flask from his desk drawer and took a slug.

"Eddie, you owe," Inky said.

"You're fired, Lautman!"

"No, I'm not," said Inky. "You need me."

"I got Litwack!"

"He ain't enough."

Gottlieb ran his hands through his hair.

He looked up.

"I figured it was easy money to get," he said.

"You don't have to pay it back," Inky said.

"How so?"

"There's more."

Inky bore the bad tidings of the whole mad plot. Gottlieb's belly boiled. He stood up and leaned forward so far it seemed like he was going to fall over his desk.

"Those goddamn Nazi twats!" he said. "I've been building this organization since before the kaiser fell! The SPHAs were turning a profit while Fritz Kuhn was still jerking off into his lederhosen! I'm not about to let a bunch of Jew-hating sauerkraut eaters bring us down!"

"They figured you'd say that," Inky said. "So they told me to torch the place and make it look like you did it for the insurance money."

"Why would they tell *you* to do that?"

"Because I work for them sometimes. On non-Jew matters."

"*What?*"

"It's a long story. Wouldn't be if you paid me more."

"You ain't gonna do it, are you?" Gottlieb said.

"I was thinking about it."

"Aw, Inky, come on."

"Give me a raise."

"I can't do that."

They went around for a while. Gottlieb got close to crying. It had been a greedy mistake, and it had backfired worse than the team car at a rest stop on the turnpike. Inky wanted to do right by him.

"All right, how about this?" Inky said. "You clear everything out of the office and make sure that Passon's does the same. At least the important stuff. That way, when we do fire the place, we don't leave anything. Then we'll scatter a bunch of evidence around that shows it's a Bund job. Like swastika patches and crazy anti-Jew notes. The papers will never blame us. They love us. So you'll get the insurance money anyway and we can pay them back with that."

Gottlieb pondered this for a second. His face brightened. Inky's plot clearly pleased him. He pounded the desk and said, "And then we'll go to Minneapolis and beat the shit out of those Aryan bastards!"

"Okay, then," said Inky.

"Keep your hands clean, Inky," said Gottlieb, who had no idea how dirty Inky's hands already were. "I'll hire my own guy."

The plan had been set in motion. Zinkoff had his doubts. And they were serious.

"But, boss," Zinkoff said, "doesn't that sound—"

"As far as I know, Zink," Gottlieb said, "I only pay you to talk on Saturday nights."

That shut Zink up. Working for Gottlieb was a pain in the ass. But it was better than the family deli.

• s i x •

THE PLAYOFFS were coming. The SPHAs needed to practice. And they practiced hard, barring the doors at the Jewish Community Center on Friday afternoons to keep out any dames who might want to distract the team with a little stocking show. Gottlieb got sweaty before the players did, screaming out orders from the sidelines like a field marshal. He'd played for fifteen years himself, and he had no qualms about grabbing a guy's elbows and forcing him into the perfect twelve-foot set form, over and over again, until the shots sank as inevitably as the *Lusitania*.

Practice usually began with court laps, twenty, thirty, forty, until Gottlieb could see substantial moisture on the players' foreheads. That was usually a sign that their egos were ready to submit to his will. After that came skill drills. The guards dribbled figure eights until they were ready to vomit, while the big men camped under the basket and locked elbows, battling for position while Gottlieb and Zinkoff lobbed bricks.

Inky and Litwack had this thing they did where they tried to get the ball past each other on the dribble, through the legs, around the back, whatever it took. Litwack had actually begun to slow down. He was saying that this would be his last season. So Inky, in his full flower, should have been able to knock him dead. But Litwack was in superb mental condition and he sometimes left Inky standing confused, driving past for an easy layup.

Fucking Litwack.

Then, usually, Gottlieb let them drink some water. After that, they practiced free throws for an hour, one hundred shots each, both baskets whooshing if it was the guards' turn and clanging if the big men shot. If you made at least eighty of your hundred, Gottlieb rewarded you by making you take another twenty. Just when you start to get good, he said, that's when you need to practice the most.

Passing drills came next, bounces and bullets, close in and crosscourt. Gottlieb positioned the SPHAs like man-sized chess pieces on a fancy hotel lawn. The ball whipped around like a top on a string. Everyone else knew that this was the part of the practice where they could go slack, as long as they made their cuts and set their picks and didn't drop the leather when it arrived. Everyone except for Inky. He handled the ball nearly all the time. There was no point in forcing a guy like Shostack to identify the open man from the top of the key. But Inky needed to know, and work, all the angles.

Shooting was easy, by comparison, except when it wasn't. They could make those two-handed set shots blindfolded. They could do this because sometimes Gottlieb made them practice while actually wearing blindfolds. If you can make a shot that way, he figured, a Rosenblum mitt in your face doesn't mean much. Today, however, he let them shoot sighted and shaved some time off the practice for accuracy. By the end, it felt like they had fifteen-pound weights tied to their hands.

The sounds of eight pairs of shoes squeaking reverberated throughout the South Philly JCC, as though the whole building were under attack by an army of giant mice. It was time for defense: foot shuffling, getting up in the face, slapping the ball away, boxing out, double-teaming, denying the passing lanes, the zone, the man-to-man, taking the charge in the two-on-one, all the groundwork needed for a hard-core SPHAs lockdown. When the SPHAs went into full defense mode, they swarmed like hornets, and the other teams might as well have been playing at a different rpm or underwater.

Gottlieb could forgive a missed shot, even an open one. A bad pass or a bungled pick got excused too, as long as they didn't happen too often. Perfect games were for Lefty Grove. But if you dropped a defensive assignment, Gottlieb would be on you at the next time-out like a slobbering dog. "In other countries, lack of effort gets Jews killed!" he'd scream, and you'd better receive that message quick, or else you'd be at the law books on Saturday nights and basketball would be relegated to the status of beloved hobby.

Finally it came time for a little four-on-four. Inky drew Sundodger and Shostack, that piece of tender musical beefsteak, for his inside guys, and Shikey Gotthofer, a rookie who couldn't hit the side of a bakery with a bag of flour, as his shooter. A strategy formed: play the in-and-out game with Sundodger, position Shostack for the putbacks, drive for layups and shoot from the top of the key, and keep the ball out of Shikey's hands. The other team had Inky's backup, Red Rosan, at the point, with Litwack on the outside drill and Fitch to get the offensive rebound if necessary. They had a different strategy. Work the ball quickly inside and kick out to Litwack when at all possible, because they knew that Shikey liked to take the double-team bait.

They had a half hour to play. Inky set his sights on a point a minute. If he could get that, then he could claim bragging rights. But Sundodger was nursing a hangover and couldn't stay with

Fitch. Shostack moved slowly as usual, and Rosan was pesky on the dribble. Inky tried gamely, made his foul shots, and had his team within four. Then Litwack caught fire and drained three sets in a row, followed by a drive past Shikey and under Shostack's hocks. After Sundodger dropped a short banker, Litwack tried that nonsense again, finding himself trapped and denied when Inky ran to the ball. Somehow Litwack worked a bullet pass between Inky's legs, a real precision move by a real pro, and found Rosan on the perimeter to drain one. It was 28–17 when the final whistle blew.

"I got nothing to say to you worms," he said, "except scram!"

The team breathed collective relief; a double practice wasn't in the offing tonight. But Inky was pissed. As usual, Litwack hadn't bragged, like the annoyingly perfect gentleman he was. Inky sopped himself off with a towel and stewed. Shostack came over.

"There's a place at the table for you tomorrow night if you want, Inky," he said.

"I'll be there," said Inky.

As the players limped out of the gym, Gottlieb pulled Inky aside, ostensibly about game strategy.

"Passon's is going up in smoke at midnight tomorrow," he said.

"Okay," said Inky.

"It's a good time. Jews make poor arson suspects on the Sabbath."

"I don't know. We light candles," said Inky.

"The *women* light candles."

"True enough."

"Still, you're gonna want to have a rock-hard alibi."

"I'll be at Shostack's," Inky said.

"His mother makes the best brisket," Gottlieb said.

She certainly did. And that was a decent draw. But Inky had other, better reasons to want to go over to Shostack's on a Friday night. Reasons that only one other person knew about. And he wanted to keep it that way.

seven

THE SHOSTACK family believed in the dictatorship of the prole-tariat, though that hadn't stopped them from buying furniture out of the Sears catalog. They lived in a lean three-story cave, 1880s vintage, near the Fifth and Wyoming trolley stop, a nice address for a family well into its third generation of citizenship. Mr. Shostack had a rock-solid tenured gig as a professor of European history at Temple, no small feat for a guy whose own parents had seen European history reflected firsthand in the blades of marauding Cossacks. They came to the States, got deloused in the shadow of the Statue of Liberty, and spent the second half of their adulthoods making damn sure their kids never had to pick up anything heavier than a book and a pen. Capitalism was so good to them that their son had been able to gallivant around St. Petersburg with Jack Reed himself and gave public lectures urg-ing crowds, impatient with news of Stalinist purges, to just give the workers' revolution a little more time.

Ma Shostack, on the other hand, came from bourgeois stock. Her people ran a butter distribution racket, and demand rarely flagged, even at the Depression's peak. She came to the marriage with a de facto dowry. Because of that, the Shostacks had plenty extra, and they only gave a small amount of it to various harmless socialist groups. Like so many, the Shostacks had found themselves gradually but willingly getting absorbed into the consumer tapestry, their ethnic edges dulled by shopping trips and viewings of *Grand Hotel* at the Coronet.

Stopping by the Shostacks' for Shabbat brought Inky welcome relief from his soot-shrouded routine. Other than a simple blessing over the candles and a *borei pri hagafen* blessing before downing a decent vintage of wine, the Shostacks eschewed religious trappings. Inky lived in a secular world, his identity unencumbered by headgear and little boxes full of sacred paper. Give him a good meal and he was satisfied.

There were five of them at table: Inky, the Shostack parents, Charlie the gentle giant, and Natalya, Charlie's younger sister (five feet four inches of creamy-skinned, naive introspection). They dined on challah and kugel and roast beef and boiled onions and some sort of crazy jelly mixed with soft-boiled eggs and creamed mustard. The conversation touched on the usual points: Hitler was a madman, and weren't the freedom fighters in Spain brave?

"The people are going to win," Natalya said. "They have to."

"I dunno," Inky said. "I've spent a lot of time hanging around 'the people.' I don't really want them in charge. After all, Hitler and Stalin were people once too."

"Stalin's just doing what he needs to in order to keep the ideals of the revolution alive," Natalya said.

"He could do it with a softer touch," Inky said.

But that was about as politically heated as things got at the table. The Shostacks were comfortable, physically and intellectually, and didn't mind it when someone challenged their political opinions. Besides, they loved Inky, and he loved them. Especially Natalya. Boy, did he ever love her, so much so that he slipped off his shoe and ran his toes up her calf and across the inside of her thigh, and she let him, while she talked excitedly about things she'd read in the *Daily Worker*. By the time Charlie was wondering aloud if he'd get to see Yehudi Menuhin play Schumann's Violin Concerto in D minor at Carnegie Hall in December, both Inky and Natalya were squirming in their seats and trying to figure out how they could get away for a while. They'd been at it for a few months now. If anyone else suspected, then they weren't talking.

After dinner, they all sat in the living room tsk-tsking the latest terrible radio news out of Europe. But in good old Roosevelt-run America, Inky was as cozy as could be, with that soft coffee-colored swirl carpet beneath his splayed hips, one arm leaning on the stuffed royal-blue armchair that could barely contain Charlie's massivity. Natalya and her ma sat on the adjacent chesterfield, Mr. Shostack in his chocolate-brown armchair with matching ottoman. The rest of the room was delicate end tables with spindly legs. Area lights brightened dark corners with passed-down art deco design. The walls were painted a mottled pink, with framed pictures of lilies or other classy-type flowers accented around. It was high middle all the way, a real *Life* magazine spread. Natalya occasionally looked at Inky with a gaze that could stop a train.

Shostack the elder's pipe ran out of juice. He needed a tobacco refill. Charlie snored gently in his chair, violin in his lap; Gottlieb's harsh drills and a bellyful of beef had really drained his tank.

"Natalya, my dear," asked the father, "would you run down to the pantry for me?"

"It's on a high shelf," she said.

"I can help," Inky said.

"Would you?" she asked.

Inky's breath was shallow, his hands shaking. She did it to him, this number with her hair in a bun and her little wool skirt, like no twist ever had before. His life with dames usually consisted of who was left over at the Bucket when the lights came on at two a.m. But Miss Shostack, recording secretary of the People's Workers Party of Northwest Philadelphia, brainy sophomore at Penn engaged deep in the study of humankind, really dizzied his birdcage.

Something about Inky's lug musk and his ball handler's dukes must have appealed to her too. The second they reached the first-floor pantry she was on him like a cat on a bowl of milk. They heaved and wrestled, jostling the dry goods.

"Oh, Inky, I'm tired of waiting for Friday nights," she said breathily as they ground their hips together hungrily, mortar seeking pestle. "I wish you'd come to party meetings with me."

He licked her neck and said, "I don't do politics. You know where I live, and you're welcome anytime."

"I'm heavily supervised here," she said.

"Tell 'em you've got a party meeting."

They locked hands, his pressing hers against the pantry wall, over their heads. Her lips opened and she gave a little moan. He'd pushed some button somewhere. She was soft and light and pliant.

"Come and see me," he said.

"Maybe…"

From the living room, Inky heard Ma Shostack yelling:

"Something is happening here!"

They unclenched, and Inky pulled a pouch of Prince Albert as they bolted from the pantry. He ran to the front door and flung it open. Bad tidings were moving through the street.

The Bund had activated. Its members traveled in numbers, dropping von Lilienfeld-Toal's vile fascist leaflets and flinging blobs of red paint at people who stood on their stoops. Inky watched as one of them strung up a man-sized rag doll with a beard, a wide-brimmed black hat, and ringlets from a nearby tree. You really had to hate Jews to hang a rabbi in effigy on Shabbat. They also drew swastikas in black chalk on the sidewalks.

Inky took a leaflet off the Shostack doorframe. On it was written "Jew Parasites Live Here," and below was a vile illustration of a long-nosed maggot, its eyes blank and hideous, as it chomped on a map of the United States. All the Jewish-owned houses in the neighborhood had gotten one. The businesses, shuttered for the Sabbath, had received a different message: "You haven't got a job. Who's got it? A Jew. How do you like it?" Inky once again found himself thinking that he was moonlighting for the wrong guys.

The Shostacks stumbled down the stairs, cursing the fascist hordes. Inky handed the old man his tobacco pouch.

"You're gonna need a smoke," he said.

"Inky," Natalya said, "aren't you going to do something?"

"Not much I can do here," he said.

"They can't get away with this. You have to stop them!"

"Seems to me it's too late to stop anything tonight," Inky said.

"Is it?" said Natalya.

A growing mob of men and some women marched down the street. They looked confident as they poured out of their houses, obviously thrilled to be strong in numbers. A kid, looking urchin-like in his short pants, stopped walking, and the crowd stopped too. But it wasn't for the kid, who couldn't have been older than twelve. The kid was carrying a wooden box. He placed it under a streetlamp, right in the middle of the crowd. The people parted as though Moses had waved his staff before them. Inky's enthusiasm dropped to zero when he realized they were stepping aside for Litwack, who mounted his pedestal like a hero.

"Fellow Jews!" Litwack said. "We cannot let this affront to our dignity stand! We have to fight back—tonight! immediately!—and show these monsters who's in charge!"

Natalya looked at Inky, and then Shostack's parents looked at Inky. Charlie bolted down the steps into the marching tide. Natalya followed him.

"Hey!" Inky shouted.

"These are our homes and businesses," Litwack was shouting. "We need to protect ourselves and our families!"

The crowd roared behind the guy, and Inky went down the steps after Shostack's sister.

"And our freedom!" Litwack shouted.

"Freedom!" the crowd said as one.

Litwack, Inky thought. *What a ball hog.*

· e i g h t ·

A FEW hours earlier, Eddie Gottlieb had been sitting in his office at Passon's, finalizing the insurance papers that would save his (and the team's) financial ass after the building burned to the ground. These were desperate times, and Gottlieb was a desperate man. Right then, six feet four inches of broad-shouldered confidence walked through the door.

"Shabbat shalom, chief," Litwack said.

"Who's the chief?" said Gottlieb. "You or me?" He tried to look nonchalant as he shoved the documents he'd been studying into a desk drawer. Litwack wouldn't have approved. He played his part straight, like Zeppo Marx.

"Let's call it a draw," Litwack said. "I don't want to bother you if you're busy."

"Don't be smart," Gottlieb said. "It's low tide. Shouldn't you be home with your family?"

"Home is two squalling toddlers and three broken ceiling fans."

"Spoken like a true family man. You want a cigar?"

"Depends on the cigar."

"Don't worry, handsome. I save the good stuff for my special dates," Gottlieb said.

"You're too good to me," Litwack replied.

Gottlieb pulled a couple of Van Dycks out of his desk drawer, did the cutting and the lighting himself, and then he and Litwack sat there puffing away as the office filled pleasantly with the aroma of cedar and toasted almond. After a few ecstatic pulls, Gottlieb spoke.

"So what brings you to my purview today, Litwack?"

"Only if you're not busy."

"I'm busy," said Gottlieb. "But not too busy for my big draw."

"Well, chief," Litwack said, "I have this concept. And I wanted to make sure that it wasn't nuts."

Litwack took a piece of paper from his breast pocket and a pen off Gottlieb's desk. He produced a quick sketch of a basketball court, with *X*s and *O*s in the appropriate quantities. "This is about defense," he said.

"The whole *game* is about defense," said Gottlieb, more than a little intrigued. What player would have the balls to chart for him? As it turned out, only two that he ever knew. But only one was ever any good at it.

Litwack had recently signed on to coach Temple's freshman team and to assist with the varsity squad. In the coming season, Stanford would be doing an East Coast swing. The Cardinals had this all-American wop named Hank Luisetti who'd developed a one-handed running shot that couldn't be stopped. In an era when an entire *team* averaged about thirty-five a night, Luisetti was averaging forty all by himself. But Litwack had a mind to stop him, and he wanted to run his strategy by Gottlieb.

Rather than playing man-to-man, which had been proving helpless against Luisetti's fancy moves, Litwack figured that the perimeter players could each guard a zone of the court near the top of the key, while the forwards stayed toward the bottom. They'd hassle whoever came into their area, but if the ball left, they'd stay put in case it returned. The center would roam the middle in case anyone got through the gauntlet. Gottlieb nearly dropped his cigar in disbelief. He'd seen zone defenses before, but this variation seemed right to him. It was so simple but so brilliant.

"I call it the box-and-one," Litwack said. "Whaddya think?"

Gottlieb thought it was the greatest thing he'd seen since Gypsy Rose Lee, but he didn't want to overplay his hand. Also, with the playoffs approaching, he wanted to use it without using it, to give Litwack credit but also to improvise on a theme. Hell, if he deployed this right, his teams might never lose again.

"Could work," Gottlieb said. "It certainly has potential."

"That's what I figured."

"I wish Lautman had come up with this the night the Bund beat the shit out of us."

"His failure was my inspiration."

Gottlieb reached into his desk drawer and fingered the insurance papers. *Maybe*, he thought, *I should tell Litwack about the whole Bund/Irish sweepstakes mess.* Litwack was righteous. He knew how to get out of trouble, and he only used his fists if he was up against a wall and someone was shouting "Jew bastard" at him. Then again, Litwack's first instinct would probably be to call in the cops, and that always made everything worse. He may have been righteous, but he was still a little politically naive. But Gottlieb had to wonder if he'd thrown his trust in with the wrong guard. Lautman almost always meant trouble. Litwack almost never did.

"That's a hell of a defense you came up with there, Harry," he said. "A hell of a defense."

In what some would call an upgrade, Harry Litwack's family had moved from Poland to Philadelphia in 1912, when Harry was five years old. At the end of the Great War, the part of Poland that Harry's parents had fled from was incorporated into the new nation of Austria. But whatever you called the area, it wasn't so great for Jews.

Harry's father, a shoemaker by trade, found plenty of work in Philadelphia, as the family settled in a neighborhood with a sizable population of door-to-door salesmen and newspaper reporters. But even though shoes were constantly in demand, the cobbler wanted his son to achieve more. He didn't understand when Harry started spending most of his waking hours shooting a ball through a peach basket. To him, sports were as bewildering as mayonnaise.

To further confuse the situation, the family spoke only Yiddish at home. The pursuit of basketball, the father said, was *meshugass*, *chazzerai*, or even worse, an *aveyre di tsayt*, translated as a "sin against time," meaning that it was a waste of time to play because the playing would amount to nothing. But Harry's father had nothing to say because the boy kept his grades high. Harry was a big star at Southern High School and then started at Temple for three seasons. By that time his father had come around. Success looked the same in any language. Litwack signed with the SPHAs the same week that Inky Lautman did, and suddenly Gottlieb had himself a backcourt of unstoppable Jews.

At every home game—and here's where Litwack drove Inky absolutely around the bend—Litwack had a Yiddishkeit cheering section that included his father, his mother, his 315-year-old grandmother, sisters, brothers, nieces, nephews, a rotating passel of aunts, uncles, cousins, second cousins, and neighbors, kids he'd coached at Temple, guys he'd played with at Temple, guys he played poker with, shopkeepers from the old neighborhood *and* the new neighborhood, and girls who wanted to sleep with him but never would because he was faithful to his wife. His wife was also there, and his kids, and his *wife*'s parents, and her aunts, uncles, cousins, second cousins, step cousins, kids from the building who were *like* cousins, and an endless stream of beloved acquaintances, friends, fans, property holders, shop-keepers, scouts, gamblers, swells, and just general Jew-loving well-wishers.

Inky had no one, except maybe the Shostacks, but even they divided their loyalties among their son, Inky, and Litwack, for-ever Litwack. He could have run for mayor if he'd wanted. Yes, he would have lost, because there was no way the town would elect a Jew mayor, but he carried enough respect so that the people would have at least given a more nuanced reason for rejecting him. In that way, Litwack represented social progress.

So it was only natural that, on that Friday night of the Bund putsch, when Litwack had been enjoying a quiet Shabbat with his family only three blocks from where Inky Lautman was feeling up Natalya Shostack in the pantry, he would end up leading the peo-ple on a march through the streets. When the activity started, the reaction was all wailing and clothes rending, but Harry Litwack would have none of that. He kissed his wife and children and went out into the street to rally his people into something above a mob, toward a higher purpose.

There must have been several dozen following Litwack down Wyoming Avenue when Inky and Natalya joined the stream.

"Inky," Natalya said, "isn't this *amazing*? We're not going to be pushed around anymore."

"Yeah, yeah, yeah," said Inky. He'd been down this path many times. The crowd got a little satisfaction, but in the morning things were always worse for the Jews.

Litwack stopped the crowd. He'd come of age between wars, but he still had military strategy down pat. The mob that wasn't really a mob numbered maybe sixty, so Litwack divided them into four divisions. Those divisions he divided into two or three platoons.

The Bund rally itself had broken up when they'd seen the response coming. Individual Bundsmen were ahead of them a few blocks, still making trouble on their way home. But Litwack and his Jews knew the neighborhood better than the Bund did. The divisions would encircle, go around blocks, head through alleyways, and engage the enemy, using superior numbers to pick them off. If the platoons caught anyone, Litwack had a strategy for capturing, which he outlined in simple detail. They wouldn't get them all, but they'd get enough. Litwack said this all so calmly that everyone obeyed. Inky would have been shouting himself hoarse into the night. How did Harry have this power over men?

As luck, fate, or design would have it, Inky and Natalya ended up in the division led by Litwack himself. They had the toughest assignment: the narrow, dirty alleys that showed up every block or so along Fourth Street. The Germans may have mistakenly called them Jew rats, but if they thought like rats, then maybe they'd have a chance to catch a predator.

Litwack pointed to Inky.

"Okay, chief, you're with me," he said.

"I think I could handle my own *platoon*, Harry," Inky said.

"I need your speed. Bring your girl too."

"She ain't my girl."

"Sure she ain't," Litwack said.

Natalya blushed. So did Inky. No one had made the connection before. Why did it have to be Litwack?

They trolled the alleys for an hour, Litwack and Inky and Natalya and a couple of other guys. Inky stepped in a puddle that didn't smell so good. He vaguely imagined that God was punishing him for having lustful thoughts on the Sabbath, but then he remembered that he didn't believe in God. The neighborhood wasn't exactly quiet—clearly the enemy had been engaged elsewhere—but their own patrol had, thus far, met with nothing but cats and garbage.

Then they saw some movement in the street up ahead, a less than subtle lumbering. Litwack gave the signal, drawing his hand through the air in the shape of a square. The two other guys went up ahead, and Litwack, Inky, and Natalya busted through the alley, fast, Litwack just a step ahead.

Within seconds, they had a fat Bundsman trapped in the box-and-one. Inky and Natalya guarded the top, the two other guys guarded the bottom, and Litwack held the middle. The guy had no way to escape the zone. He dashed toward Natalya's corner, mistakenly thinking that she might be the weakest, but Litwack and Inky collapsed on him fast, and then Natalya had her toes in his gut and the bastard fell to his knees.

In the streetlight, Inky saw his face.

Helmut.

"Hey, Inky," Helmut said.

"You *know* him?" Natalya said.

"I know a lot of guys," said Inky.

"Playing for the home team tonight, eh, Inky?" Helmut said.

Inky slapped him hard across the mouth.

"Don't talk to me like that," Inky said.

"You're a real tough guy, Lautman."

Litwack said, with quiet righteousness, "I suppose you think *you're* the tough guy, making women and children afraid in their own homes on a Friday night."

"Not me," Helmut said. "I just go where the Bund tells me."

"Well," Litwack said, "I tell you to go to hell."

Litwack brought both fists down on the back of Helmut's head, hard enough to make the German collapse completely. Helmut's whole body lay splayed on the pavement. He was definitely not available for further crimes that night.

"I thought you said we were going to take them in quietly," Natalya said.

"Sometimes you take them quietly, and sometimes you beat the shit out of them," Litwack said. "It's situational."

Litwack, Inky thought. *You have to respect the guy.* It drove him crazy.

· n i n e ·

INKY LAY on his bed, smoking a Viceroy. That had been quite an evening. Inches away from something very strange and beautiful in a pantry, he'd suddenly found himself in the middle of both a pogrom and a vigilante hunt. It might have occurred to him that the whole megillah was very American, that he was fortunate to live in a land where the oppressor could turn into the hunted on a dime. But he didn't tend toward those kinds of thoughts. Mostly Inky thought about the Bund's stupidity. Why would the Bundsmen hit a densely populated neighborhood where they knew everyone was home, many of them drunk, and many of those drunken people either armed or at the very least good with their fists? Did they really think they had a chance to get out without out a beating?

If I'd been in charge of the Bund, Inky thought, *I would have run things better.* But of course he wouldn't have been in charge of the Bund, because why would he have been? The worst thing that Inky could say about his own people was that they talked too much and their houses sometimes smelled like cabbage; that was hardly grounds for an organized campaign of racial hatred. He'd no sooner distribute propaganda depicting Jews as worms than he would go to confession on Sunday. The Jews weren't taking anyone's jobs. They were either making their own jobs or doing jobs that the Bund and its supporters couldn't do because they weren't smart enough. Inky just wanted to get paid and stay out of the way.

At the same time, Inky found himself grinding his teeth at the neighborhood's response. Of course those people had been in the moral right, and what they'd done was certainly better than weeping or, worse, calling the cops. But there'd been something almost too calculated in the countermob's actions, like they'd been waiting for something like this to go down. These weren't scared peasants or powerless intellectuals. Not really. Not anymore. They were so ready to *play* the victim that they almost *weren't* victims. Litwack, in particular, had talked and acted as though he'd been rehearsing in front of the bathroom mirror. Inky had followed Litwack reluctantly because circumstances had forced him to do so. That had made him unhappy enough, but the real problem wasn't that he was following a man—even one he resented for semilegitimate reasons—it was that he'd felt like he was following a *script*. The Bund had written the first act, and Litwack had written the second. They hadn't consulted or colluded, but they'd done exactly what the other had wanted. Inky felt like he was a bench player in a game whose result had been decided long ago. And that wasn't a feeling he liked.

The cigarette had burned to its nub, so Inky lit another. He allowed himself one smoke for anxiety. After that, he turned his thoughts to sex. Specifically, he thought about what Natalya's thighs would look like if he could ever get the wool skirt down to her ankles. *Young*, he thought. *Smooth. Dark but not too dark*.

He didn't have to wonder for long.

Someone knocked at midnight; Inky figured it was Joe from downstairs, looking for him to rough up a patron. Inky usually pulled closing time duty on Fridays. Instead, he opened it and there she stood, her blouse damp with sweat, a couple of strands of hair loosened from the bun.

"It's you," he said.

"Who else could it be?" Natalya said.

"A lot of people."

"Women?"

"Some."

"Like me?"

"Not like you," Inky said.

Natalya seemed to enjoy that.

"So why tonight?" Inky added.

"We had some unfinished business."

"A girl shouldn't come to this neighborhood alone."

"I took a taxi."

"Still."

"Still?"

"Still," he said and pulled her close for a kiss.

When that was done, she said, "They all got drunk and fell asleep at home."

"Who could blame 'em?" Inky said. "That was some scene."

"But I didn't want to drink. So I escaped instead."

Inky swept his arm across his body, the maître d' at the world's grimiest restaurant.

"Do come in," he said.

She looked around. A half-eaten chicken sat on the table, attracting flies. Beer bottles and cigarette butts lay where they'd fallen. Train vibrations shook the room, causing the lights to flicker.

"God, Inky, this place is a pit," she said.

"I'm only here while they finish the renovations on the country house," he said.

"You could use a woman."

"In a lot of ways."

"Don't take that wrong."

"Oh, I don't."

He looked at her. She looked at him. Their eyes measured the situation. They froze time. For years, they'd ached for each other. Now that itch would get scratched, but they both knew it wouldn't happen lightly. Sometimes when you scratch, you feel better. But sometimes you just bleed.

Inky reached around and caught the zipper of her skirt. She moaned a little, in a way that said, "Do it and don't turn back." The zipper went down, the wool dropped, and there stood Natalya in her panties and hose, skirt bunched over her shoes, which she slipped off easily. Next, Inky put a hand on each thigh and snapped the garters. She gasped as he rolled down the hose, real slow. When that was done, he stepped back and looked down. Her thighs didn't disappoint. And they were his for the taking.

The two of them panted. When he kissed her neck, she arched with a moan. She moved her hand lightly across his waist. Inky wanted more. He grabbed her hand and she moaned again. "Undo my buttons," he said. She did, and he showed her what he wanted, squeezes up and down, while he undid her blouse and started running his tongue across her collarbone. Sweat formed on her temples. She looked at him with soft brown eyes, biting her lower lip for emphasis. Inky didn't need persuading.

He pushed her onto the bed. Natalya drew up her knees. Inky knelt on the floor beside her. Rough splinters jabbed his shins. But it was the best angle for what he wanted to do. He licked her ankles and her calves. Damn it, she had great legs. He wanted to eat them. So he did, working over her thighs like a kid on a double-chocolate ice cream cone. She tasted sweet and salty.

He stood up, rolled his pants down to his ankles, and got on the bed next to her. They pressed closer and grabbed each other. Natalya made noises. She clawed at his back. He straddled her and bent forward, sucking her little round brown nipples.

"Do it, Inky," Natalya said.

He mounted her. She wrapped her legs around his waist and arched her back. Inky grunted softly, but then she started grinding her hips in a circle and he was moaning too. Usually with the hookers he picked up downstairs, he could slap thighs for thirty minutes. On a good night, it was a quarter hour before he started feeling anything at all. But Natalya wasn't going to let him have that much time. Where had she learned these moves? From a book?

They went at it, hard, for three minutes that seemed like three years. Something powerful rose inside him. He snarled like a silverback gorilla. She shrieked vibrato.

Then it was done, and then they rolled apart.

"Holy nuts," Inky said.

All over the city, the country, and the world, people were weeping into their pillows, for reasons grand and small, but not in that bed and not on that night. Inky and Natalya lay together, sweaty and alive. The elevated rumbled past. A dirty wind came through the open window and blew over them. In the street, someone broke a bottle.

"Inky?" she asked.

"What, baby?" he said.

"Were you scared tonight?"

"Not really."

"Me neither."

"Yeah?"

"The Bund doesn't scare me."

"They should scare you a little."

"Why?" Natalya asked. "They're just thugs."

"They got numbers."

"Yes, well, I'm tired of being afraid."

"That's good."

"I want to fight. Some students at Penn have started a league."

"What, like a basketball league?"

"No, a league for Jews to defend themselves."

"So it *is* like a basketball league."

"This is different. We attack first."

"Whaddya mean?" Inky asked.

"I mean we find the Bund and attack them, where they work, where they live. To let them know what it's like."

"That doesn't sound like a good idea."

"Are we supposed to sit back and take it?"

"We're not taking it," Inky said. "But we're not dishing it out, either. Believe me, being the tough guy ain't no fun."

"You're some pacifist," she said. "Mister Beat-People-Up-for-Money."

He instinctively drew his fist back to strike. But she didn't flinch. She knew he wouldn't hurt anyone unless he was getting paid.

"I believe my point has been made," she said.

"Goddammit," he said.

Why did chicks always want to talk after fucking? And why did *everyone* always want to talk about politics? Inky wanted a beer, real bad. So he went to the icebox and got one.

"You got one for me?" Natalya asked.

"I don't," Inky said. "But you can share mine."

They alternated slugs. That malt, however stale, felt cool and smooth going down.

"What are we going to do about the Bund?" Natalya said.

There she went again.

"Ain't much to do," Inky said.

"But they're a menace, Inky. They have to be stopped."

"Time has a way of stopping everyone."

"That's a cowardly answer, Inky."

"I'm no coward," Inky said. "I just don't like big commitments."

She was passionate. "Jews have to get the fight in them," she said. "Germany looks hopeless, but we can win in the States."

The strong would lift up the weak and someday there'd be a state of Israel where all Jews would live harmoniously in a workers' paradise.

"Can't we just move to the Main Line or something?" Inky said. "They got grass out there."

She smacked his shoulder.

"You're unbelievable," she said.

"You ain't seen unbelievable yet," Inky said.

He moved in for seconds. She served them. They were good.

· ten ·

NATALYA LEFT before dawn. Inky offered to take her home, but she said she didn't want to disturb the Spartan at rest. Maybe he should have insisted, but honestly, he was so tired and sore that he could barely move. But he didn't need to worry. She was tougher than the boiled meat that Joe served downstairs.

It was well past noon when Inky heard a pounding at his door. He thought it might come off its hinges again. Just once, he wanted to wake up normally. The bartender was shouting:

"You got a phone call, Lautman!"

At least Inky hadn't woken with a hangover. Usually he needed to stick his head in the deep freeze for a few minutes before he could even walk straight. The team bus was leaving at two for a six p.m. game in Paterson, a real glamorous place. The game had originally been scheduled in Philly, but the Broadwood booked an Artie Shaw concert. That didn't come around every weekend.

It was time to face the ding-dong day. Inky got up, got dressed, threw his uniform and a spare shirt in his duffel, and went down to the bar. The Bucket was lit the same no matter the hour. Even at noontime, it looked like streetlamp beams were coming through the shutters. A thin film of dust covered every surface, and no amount of mopping could clear out the stink in the air. Joe said the smell gave his drinks character.

He had a phone in the back room, which was piled high with jazz records and newspapers dating back from before Inky knew how to read.

Gottlieb was on the line, his voice as shrill as a fire alarm.

"Lautman!" he shrieked.

"Good morning, Eddie."

"Get down here!"

"Get down where?"

"To Passon's!"

Inky lowered his voice.

"I thought Passon's got torched."

"Just come over now!"

"Only if you buy me breakfast."

"You can eat my ass for breakfast!"

"Sunny side up," Inky said. "I'll be there in half an hour."

Inky kept his word. When he arrived at Passon's, he found Gottlieb sitting in a chair at his intact desk. The walls of the office had browned, like toast left in too long. A smell of charred paper gave the air a slightly toxic bent. There were water stains on the wall and little puddles on the floor. The floor felt warmer than usual under Inky's feet. Gottlieb had his head in his hands and moaned softly.

"Eddie," Inky said.

Gottlieb raised his head.

"Those," he said, in a near whisper, and then, his voice rising to a nasty pitch, "incompetent, motherfucking, cocksucking, two-balled bitches! Anyone with half a brain should be able to burn down a building. I never should have hired guys off the docks!"

"Sometimes, Eddie, I wonder if you think things through."

"I got a lot on my mind," Gottlieb said, "like how to get you shrimp dicks to Jersey by sundown!"

"We'll get there," Inky said.

Gottlieb sighed.

"We're gonna have to take a dive in Minnesota," he said. "Or the Bund will own us."

Gottlieb looked like his heart was about to explode. Then again, he usually did. He sat there, making his calculations. Minnesota. That would be a long, brutal drive. It would take a round of exhibition games to afford the trip across the Mississippi. And they still had the playoffs ahead of them.

"Things will work out," Inky said.

Gottlieb pounded the desk.

"Fuck fuck fuckety fuck fuck fuck!" he said.

With two minutes left in the first half, the Crescents were up by five. Their point guard had been poking Inky in the eye all night. Either the refs weren't looking or they'd been paid not to see. Either way, Inky couldn't move the ball around with that spider in his face. Passes went into the stands and shots were bouncing off the side of the rim. Litwack was hot, though, and kept the SPHAs in the game. The usual Litwack.

Kaselman grabbed the ball after a Paterson clang and got it up court. Inky saw a wedge in the right lane. He drove. His defender shuffled alongside him like a dog trying to hump a pillow. Inky had to get this barnacle off his hull. He hopped, shuffled his right foot before his left, scooped the ball under the defender's outstretched arm, and flipped it upward. Inky could see that it was headed for the net, though he didn't see all the way because an elbow crashed into the bridge of his nose. Inky fell to the floor, eyes closed, little purple dots flowing around the periphery of his vision. A whistle blew.

"Traveling!" said the ref.

Gottlieb exploded off the bench like a rocket on Chinese New Year's. Inky got to his feet and wasn't much calmer. It felt like there'd been a mining disaster in his sinus cavity.

"I was foulded!" Inky said.

"Foulded?" said the ref.

"Whubdever!" Inky said. "You knub what I'm talking about."

Gottlieb arrived, clearly prepared to argue until he headed for the lockers. Getting ejected didn't bother him. The SPHAs had already clinched the playoffs. He had an appointment with a bucket of booze.

"You fucking mongoloid!" he roared. "Didja see that guy almost take off Inky's nose? That's a big nose too!"

"Hey!" Inky said.

By this time, the crowd was starting to get agitated. The SPHAs buzzed around the bench like angry hornets, except for Litwack, who sat there coolly, arms crossed, superior. The ref tossed Gottlieb with a showy gesture. Then, just to make things interesting, he tossed Inky too. As Gottlieb left the court, he flipped the clipboard Litwack's way.

"You're in charge," he said. "Beat these guys."

Litwack put on a scheme where he controlled the ball from the high post. He had the SPHAs tied by the half. When they got to the locker room, Gottlieb was already drunk and Inky was wearing a towel.

"We caught 'em, boss," Litwack said.

"Good for you!" Gottlieb said. "I'm busy right now."

"You can always count on Harry," Inky said.

"I don't need any lip, Lautman. I just want to get out of this so we can get back home to our wives…Oh, wait, I forgot. You don't have a wife."

"I roam free," Inky said.

"I don't have a wife either," Shostack added unhelpfully.

"You're so perfect, Litwack. Such a team player," Inky said. "But you didn't seem to give a shit when I was down."

"You traveled," Litwack said.

"Oh really?"

"I saw it."

"You saw nothing."

"I went to see your mother in the nuthouse. I fucked her good too."

Inky whipped off his towel and lunged for Litwack's throat. The whole team caught him. He snarled and thrashed.

"Don't you talk about my mother!" Inky said.

The woman was stone trash, but Inky would defend her to the root of his soul if Litwack was leveling the insult.

Gottlieb stood.

"GODDAMMIT!" he shouted.

This got their attention.

"There are more important things in the world. Harry, shut the fuck up and run the team. Inky, you be a man. You two are the best basketball players in the world who don't play for the Harlem Rens. If you can't get along, then I'm gonna go sell insurance."

"You got no heart," Inky growled at Litwack.

"You got no soul," Litwack responded.

Gottlieb raised his flask and said, "If I keep drinking this shit, I'll have no hair on my balls."

Halftime was over. Paterson, an inferior team in most every way, didn't have a prayer in the back nine. The SPHAs won easily, 39–26. Inky didn't feel like driving home with the team. He figured he'd catch a cab to the bus station and then get the ten p.m. But no one ever punched his ticket.

That night, Inky was destined to take a rougher ride.

· eleven ·

INKY GOT dressed and went outside. He lit a Viceroy. A sedan pulled alongside him. The window rolled down. It was Kunze.

"Quite a display there, Lautman," he said.

"I'm an entertainer," said Inky. "First and foremost."

"I saw there was a fire at Passon's last night. Too bad it didn't go all the way. Your boss could use the money."

"Yeah, well..."

"We've got the docks in our pocket, Inky. Bad place to hire a pro-Jew arsonist."

"Clearly."

"So I take it you're going to play our little game in Minnesota, then."

"Talk to Gottlieb."

"We'd rather talk to you."

"I'm busy," Inky said.

"We've got a little party to take you to," said Kunze.

"I don't like parties."

"You'll like this one."

"Nah."

Inky turned around in time for Gerhard to hit him square in the face with a garbage can lid. He felt his remaining nose cartilage give way. As he dropped to his knees, he figured he'd be going to that party after all.

Inky sat next to Helmut. The kraut prodded a gat into Inky's left kidney. Kunze and the Estonian count sat in the front, looking smug. The count was driving. They'd generously given Inky a piece of tape for his nose. It still looked (and felt) like someone had stuck his face in a meat grinder.

They drove the twenty or so miles into Manhattan and then a bunch of blocks more. With traffic, it took them well over an hour. Finally, just as Inky was considering passing out, they pulled up in front of the Hotel New Yorker, a forty-three-story art deco temple on Eighth Avenue. Inky knew the address because Fitch had stayed there once with his band, and Fitch told the team that they'd seen Garbo, or someone who'd looked like Garbo, in the lobby. Inky was impressed, but not too impressed. Garbo wasn't his type. He had a weird thing for Myrna Loy.

Kunze slipped the doorman a fiver to park the car.

"Nice to see the Bund spending wisely," Inky said.

"Can it, Lautman," said Helmut.

The elevator went all the way up to the thirty-sixth floor. They walked down the hall to a door marked Private Dining Room. Inside, a jowly little man (because, in the end, they were all little men, and the higher their stature, the littler they were) wearing thin-rimmed round glasses sat there, gorging on the remains of a roasted chicken.

"Ah, Kunze," he said. "I was wondering if you'd gotten lost."

Kunze gave him a salute. Helmut and the count followed.

"Of course not, *mein Führer*," Kunze said.

Mine what? thought Inky. *This ain't no Führer.*

"I've brought you a special guest," said Kunze.

Gerhard shoved Inky forward.

"This is Inky Lautman, perhaps the second-best Jewish basketball player in the world."

Fucking Litwack.

"He also works for us."

"I'm off duty tonight," Inky said.

The little man rose from his chair and extended his hand.

"It is a pleasure to meet someone who realizes the inferiority of his people," he said.

"That's not putting it right," said Inky.

"My name," said the little man, "is Fritz Julius Kuhn."

German born in 1896, Kuhn, much like another führer of note, had won the Iron Cross for bravery in a losing infantry cause during the Great War. After the Armistice, but not because of it, Kuhn entered the University of Munich, earning a degree in chemical engineering. He spent the rich end of the 1920s in Mexico, exploiting resources, drinking mescal, and fucking prostitutes. When that well ran dry, Kuhn moved to the United States, getting a job, not surprisingly, at the Ford Motor Company, becoming a naturalized citizen in 1934. But thoughts of a Jewless Germany were never far from his heart.

Here's how the Nazis came to America: In 1933, an unemployed syphilitic named Heinz Spanknobel, excited by Hitler's rise to power in Germany, formed, with the blessing of Deputy Führer Rudolf Hess, a domestic society initially called Friends of the Hitler Movement. That got really bad press, so they changed it to Friends of the New Germany. The group claimed to exist to spread the German culture and language throughout the backward-thinking, moderately progressive United States, but instead mostly served to distribute cartoon pamphlets that depicted Jews as vermin, a type of pamphlet that Inky knew all too well. Fortunately for America's Jews, Spanknobel was a total dope and got deported in October 1933 for failing to register as an agent of the German government.

With domestic fascism suffering from a bit of a leadership gap, the American Nazi Party, headed by a Chicago-based German citizen named Fritz Gissibl, took over. He appointed his deputy, Walter Kappe, to run the day-to-day operations. They ordered all male members of the organization, numbering between five and ten thousand, to wear a white shirt and black trousers, topped with a black hat festooned with a red symbol. The ladies wore a white blouse and a black skirt. Membership was largely restricted to the fashion-forward cities of New York and Chicago. (Later, Kappe returned to Nazi Germany, where he organized two four-man teams of saboteurs to invade and infiltrate the American government. They were all arrested upon arrival in the States, stripped of every right known to man and some unknown, and executed to the general glee of the war-weary citizenry.)

Even Hitler could see that these guys didn't have the stuff. He ordered the Friends of the New Germany disbanded, to be replaced by a new organization, das Amerikadeutscher Volksbund, or Bund for short. In March 1936, the Bund was consecrated on Hitler's order. For some reason, he ordered it consecrated in Buffalo, New York. Fritz Julius Kuhn took over and then caught the first boat to Berlin, where the Olympics were about to go down.

Somehow Kuhn had wrangled an invite to a party at Hitler's private estate. A few phone calls found him the best Berlin hooker that twenty bucks could buy. They shared a bottle of schnapps and hired a cab, which cost more than the hooker.

At the door, they announced him:

"Fritz Julius Kuhn, of das Amerikadeutscher Volksbund, and his...companion."

He entered and they presented him with a glass of fresh champagne, which he definitely didn't need.

"Where is my leader?" Kuhn roared. "Where is my führer?"

Hitler, as it happened, was standing nearby, being political. The ruckus called him over. He prepared to summon his personal guard.

"I'm sorry, who are you?" he asked.

"I'm your American counterpart," Kuhn said, suppressing a belch. "The leader of the Bund!"

Der Führer sighed. Couldn't he get one competent emissary in America? That was all he asked.

"Please keep your voice down," Hitler said. "There are other guests."

"They should be grateful to be here at all!" Kuhn said. "Soon they will be crushed under our mighty boot, and—"

"That is enough!"

Kuhn woke on his hotel bed the next morning with a terrible hangover and a lump on his head the size of Poland. Also, the hooker had taken his wallet. He stayed in Germany for the entire Olympics, though he never got to pay obeisance again. He still returned home, drunk with both spirits and power, under the impression that he was Germany's favorite American son. Now he could boast a following in the high five digits, largely kept afloat by his effective Philadelphia PR arm.

Inky Lautman sat across the table from Kuhn, eating. Inky had been hungry and he'd plowed in, even though they'd brought him, on purpose, a big ham steak with mashed potatoes. If they thought that this Jew was going to turn down a platter of pork, then they had the wrong idea about Jews in general.

"So, if I may ask…" Inky said.

"You may," said Kuhn.

"To what do I owe this unexpected luxury vacation?"

"Because, Unky, Kunze wanted you to see the rise of a new America."

"Inky," said Inky.

"Inky?"

"My name is Inky."

"What does that mean?"

"It means what it means."

"A Jew rat name."

Inky threw a bone at Kuhn's chest. The American führer flinched.

"Inky has a temper, which is why we like him," Kunze said.

"He is insolent, like all his people," said Kuhn.

"You smell like hops," Inky said.

"Sit him in the front row tomorrow night," said Kuhn. "And keep a gun on him."

"What's tomorrow night?" Inky said.

"The beginning of the end for your kind," said Kuhn. "You'll see."

That doesn't sound good, Inky thought. *But at least I'll have a front-row seat.*

· twelve ·

INKY SPENT the night at the Belvedere Hotel, courtesy of the Bund. He ordered room service and charged it to Kuhn, didn't eat anything, and then ordered another meal, which he did eat, along with a fifth of scotch, which he drank. It was noon, glorious noon, when he woke. He took a long bath, because he could, and then ordered more room service and more scotch.

Leaving the room was out of the question, because they had a thug standing across the hall, Helmut alternating with a guy who looked like Helmut. But on the shift change, Inky slipped out, went downstairs, bought a newspaper, and got a haircut in the hotel salon, also charged to the Bund. It was a pretty nice day all in all; a freebie is a freebie no matter who's footing the tab. He went back up to the room, because cutting out would have been rude. Besides, he wanted to see whatever he was supposed to see that night.

They came to get him at dusk.

"Time for the party," Kunze said.

"And here I am without a thing to wear," said Inky. "Where are we going?"

"Madison Square Garden."

That's some party, Inky thought.

They hit the streets like sailors on shore leave. The sidewalks were more crowded than usual on Eighth Avenue; it had been a trickle at first, but soon the crowd thickened, and it was growing noticeably more Jewish. How could Inky tell they were Jewish? He could tell. A steady stream of his people moved past him. They were holding signs, many of them hand printed, protesting the Bund. Inky found himself growing disoriented.

Then the chant started:

"Down with the bund! Down with the Bund! Down with the Bund!"

Inky wanted to say, "I got three Bund right here, two of them major officials, and you can have them for supper." But Helmut's gun in his side gave him the sense not to speak.

"What is this?" he said.

"This," said Kunze, "is the night America has been waiting for."

The outside of the Garden came into full view. A mob several thousand strong had formed a hundred yards from the main doors, near the intersection of Fiftieth and Eighth. They were braying for blood. The cops had set up a barricade, beating back the occasional line charges with shoves, whistles, and rough hands. On the other side of the street there were Nazis, or at least Bund members, bleating for the opposite.

Both sides were throwing cans and hurling profanities. The Jewish side started chanting, "It won't happen here! It won't happen here!" Their counterparts, like schoolboys with an inadequate response to a taunt, chanted back, "Yes, it will! Yes, it will!"

"This is nuts," Inky said.

"You're a witness to history, Inky," Kunze said. "With a front-row seat. Tonight the Bund will rise."

"You look pretty outnumbered to me," Inky said.

"Ah, but you haven't been inside yet," said von Lilienfeld-Toal.

Mayor Fiorello LaGuardia, showing some knowledge of the Constitution, had blessed this affair in the press. "It would be a strange thing indeed if I should make any attempt to prevent this meeting just because I don't agree with the sponsors," he said to the papers. "I would then be doing exactly as Adolf Hitler is doing in carrying on his abhorrent form of government." This would be the Bund's night of glory, and the city was superficially on its side. For now.

Inky and his captors swung to the crowd's left, looking like civilians, neutral. No one bothered them. They walked to the side of the arena, through an unmarked door, and down some metal stairs. It was the first time Inky had ever been inside Madison Square Garden. He would have rather it had been for a heavyweight fight or, God willing, a basketball game. But this also had a strange appeal.

In the rear of the stage, lit by a full spot, stood a sixty-foot-tall banner bearing the image of George Washington. The Father of Our Country had his right hand in his left coat pocket. He gazed serenely toward the rafters, oblivious to how his image was being manipulated. Loyal Bund members filled every seat. The Garden echoed with their collective roar.

In front of the cardboard General Washington stood a few dozen loyal soldiers wearing the full Bund uniform. They pounded on drums hung around their necks. More loyalists marched down the aisles to take their places behind the drummers. They were young and newsreel friendly. Half of them carried the American flag and half of them carried the Nazi swastika. They lined up behind a rostrum of Roman-style columns. To Inky's eyes, history looked a lot weirder than the books made it sound.

A fat woman sang "The Star-Spangled Banner." The crowd sang along. At a Phillies game, that song sounded sweet and innocent, like a child's nursery rhyme. In this setting, it seemed like the herald of the world's end, especially when followed by a rousing, deafening chorus of "Deutschland Über Alles." Inky felt something bad stirring in his gut.

When the song ended, Fritz Julius Kuhn entered the arena, puffed with pride and wearing shoes that added two inches to his height. People bellowed his name. Tonight would be his coronation. He ascended the podium and delivered the *heil.* Nineteen thousand people heiled back, and Inky got a chill. He looked around. He was sitting on the floor of a Madison Square Garden festooned with swastikas. *The Bund may be a joke*, he thought, *but there are a lot of people in here.*

Kunze leaned over toward Inky and said, "This is going to be good."

"It's going to be something," Inky said.

Kuhn waited for the crowd to quiet, and then he began:

"Before you, you see the majesty of George Washington, the American Cincinnatus. When General Washington gave his first farewell speech to the nation, he spoke of his greatest fear: that America should become entangled in foreign affairs. Yet President Rosenfeld, with his Jew Deal, is threatening to do just that, by meddling in the affairs of the great sovereign nation of Germany. He would do well to heed the words of George Washington, lest he face the wrath of the people who elected him in the first place!"

To Inky, this sounded like the incoherent ranting of a stupid, pandering man. But the crowd went nuts. It was nothing compared to what followed.

"Now," Kuhn said, "the Bund is fighting shoulder to shoulder with patriotic Americans to protect America from a race that is not the American race, that is not even a white race…"

Inky's fist began to clench and unclench. As Kuhn's speech went on, the calumnies continued to mount, each lie bigger than the next: The Jews controlled everything, they cost "the white man" his job, all Jews were Communists, and Christ was not a Jew. But when Kuhn said, "The Jews are enemies of the United States," Inky went over the edge.

"No we ain't!" he shouted. A quick elbow to Helmut's ribs jostled the gun away, and Inky found himself running toward the wall, hands shaking, shocked to find his eyes filled with tears of rage.

"You Nazi motherfuckers!" he shouted. "We will *bury* you!"

The Bundsmen were off the stage and on Inky fast, raining blows to his midsection and his head. They went at him hard. He slipped around like a fish on deck and got in a couple of shots, but as the punches and kicks started to accumulate, he felt himself blacking out fast. *It all ends here*, he thought.

An army of New York's finest burst through the side doors. They charged the stage. Inky's assailants suddenly had other problems. The Bundsmen raised their arms against a rain of truncheons, while on stage Kuhn continued to scream against the "Jew interlopers" who were trying to destroy the American way of life.

It seemed Inky's limbs still worked. There was light by the side door, and he crawled toward it. He saw Kunze and the count sliding past, unruffled, working their way toward backstage and safety. Suddenly, Helmut was moving toward him. Helmut grabbed Inky's leg, pulled him backward, and crawled up Inky's body like a tiger about to have his supper. Somehow Inky flipped over and got Helmut off him. They both found their feet. Helmut raised his gun, ready to fire. Inky didn't see a way around the bullet. He hoped Helmut's aim was as bad as his breath.

A cop caught Helmut on the back of the head. The German's skull opened like a rotten melon. Blood sprayed everywhere. The cop gestured toward the side door, toward air.

"Get outta here!" he shouted.

Inky took stock. Nothing had been broken. But he still felt pretty bad, even worse than after one of Gottlieb's double practices. He made his way to the door and pushed through into the night.

Thousands of jeering Jewish protesters berated the cops, screaming for Nazi blood. Inky saw a bunch of them charge a cop and knock him off his horse. One of them mounted and took a ride around the perimeter. Someone handed the Jew rider a burning Nazi flag. He took off down Eighth Avenue, pursued by a half dozen mounted police. Just another night in New York City.

Inky had seen enough. He lurched toward Penn Station. Kunze had funded his little vacation, so he had enough money in his pocket to catch a train. His lips were swollen and bloody, his body bruised, his shirt torn. He looked like any guy coming home to Philly after a rough weekend away.

He got a seat on the last train out. Someone had left a newspaper. Inky read the front page. It seemed that, in Germany, the Nazis had been busy. They'd busted into synagogues and hauled women out. There were burnings and assaults and midnight abductions. Inky suddenly saw the whole evil plot unfolding. These weren't just bumblers with a fat checkbook. They were dangerous, strong, and crazy. And they could win. *There's no way we can let those bastards beat us at basketball*, he thought. *Or at anything else.*

He wasn't neutral anymore.

PART TWO

1938

· t h i r t e e n ·

WINTER CAME. The city gave in to the cold and the wet like a helpless wino getting rolled in the shipyards. A tragic layer of dark-gray sleet coated the streets. The wireless carried nothing but news of war, and every day that news got worse. Hitler treated the world like his dog, and dust gathered in America's belly. No one had any money, and death was in the air.

After what he'd seen at Madison Square Garden, Inky had stopped working for the Bund. He felt good about this decision. But it also meant he was a little light in the shoebox at the end of every month, so he stopped eating meat unless someone else was buying. Meanwhile, Litwack got an honorary degree from Temple, even though he'd only received his actual degree a few years before; Gottlieb had a minor heart attack that he didn't tell anyone about; Zink ate an entire cheesecake one night after Gottlieb yelled at him; Fitch took the orchestra to Atlantic City; Shostack practiced the violin; Natalya became the recording secretary for

Students for a New American Society; and the SPHAs marched through the Eastern League with single-minded precision, a reverse jackboot of basketball dominance. Everything may have been going to shit in Europe and beyond, but that didn't prevent good ball movement, swarming defense, and a well-timed elbow to the chops from winning lots of games. One more win and the title belonged to them. Again.

But it had to go through New York. *Always New York*, Gottlieb moaned to himself in those private moments when everyone but he and the raccoons in Fairmount Park was asleep. He'd had to put up with New York his whole life. That damn city was always trying to top you. If you said you'd shot at a peach basket as a kid, some schmuck from the Bowery would counter with the bottom rung of a fire escape, or a garbage can, or they said that they'd used rolled-up socks as balls when times were tough. He'd heard all about the tight quarters and the matchbox-sized gyms. *But also*, he thought, *the Lower East Side isn't so rough. At least if you're there, you get to live in New York.*

You know what? Gottlieb thought. *Fuck New York. Try spending a few months in Philadelphia and see how you like your life then. We've got all the soot, all the dirt, all the bums, all the corruption, and all the venereal disease that New York has, but we ain't got DiMaggio or Broadway. Our dames are shorter and maybe not as smart, and lots of them are Catholic. It's a real shit sandwich without the trimmings. But we still wake up in the morning, or sometimes the afternoon.*

Gottlieb knew that New York churned out good basketball. He'd seen the Brownsville Dux (pronounced "Dukes" but spelled with an *x* because they wanted you to know that they were uneducated and therefore authentic street) play all comers at Washington Bath on Coney Island. He'd toured Appalachia with the Roosevelt City Five. He'd experienced the legend of Nate Hertzman firsthand, sitting on the opposing bench the day that Hertzman, the star of the Original Celtics, faced an entire arena of drunken hooligans. That place had been louder than an AFL-CIO rally the weekend before Election Day. But Hertzman was a cold, merciless bastard. He stared at the crowd with a face of stone for several minutes, daring them to pelt him with bottles. They yelled profanities at him that they only marched out on special occasions. He turned on his heel toward the hoop, asked for the ball, bounced it once, and shot it up and through without even a thought of it touching the rim. Then he turned back toward the crowd and pulled down his pants to show off his elegantly circumcised schlong, opening his arms to the sky and opening the gates of hell. The crowd poured down in a wave of hate that sent Gottlieb hiding under the bleachers and sent Hertzman to the hospital with two bruised kidneys. But he'd gone a winner.

Hertzman always stole the headlines, Hertzman, who learned his ballhandling skills by dribbling from his tenement around the horse-drawn carts and the pickle vendors all the way to Seward Park so he could play pickup games of one-on-one for a nickel or an ice cream cone. He made sure that all the reporters knew all that stuff, and he had taken more than one of them on a tour through the old neighborhood, planting friendly faces on the court to make sure he gave the lasting impression of eternal schoolyard legend. As a teammate of his once said, Hertzman "could pass a ball through a keyhole." That phrase had appeared in more newspaper stories than "a chicken in every pot." But the keyhole didn't make him any less of an asshole. Gottlieb knew that underneath all the tender, hardscrabble, up-from-the-ghetto stories lay the soul of a man who liked to hurt. Sometimes parts of Gottlieb's body still ached from when Hertzman had elbowed him on the court. Bruises have long memories.

And now Gottlieb had to coach against the guy too, had to hear about his tactical skills like he was the Duke of Wellington at

Waterloo instead of just a street kid with an innate sense of when to perform the give-and-go and when to talk to hacks. This was all fine, as it went. It wouldn't be a game without competition. But Gottlieb hated not getting credit. He had ideas too, he had innovations, he had the *naches* to implement them, and he had the roster.

Hertzman could teach his men a lot of skills, maybe more, in the end, than Gottlieb could. But he couldn't teach them the winner's most important quality: resentment. Even though he hadn't had it too great, he'd still had it too good. Gottlieb sensed a subtle softness in Hertzman and his teams, not detectable to the untrained basketball eye. That's why Gottlieb loved Inky Lautman. Inky carried more resentment within his blood than a thousand lovers spurned.

Even Litwack, who seemed to cruise through life with princely ease, kept a secret store of bitterness that he could draw upon in the fourth quarter, when the game was tight and the opposing knees were headed toward your nut sack. They were all from Philly, and being from Philly bred resentment. *Fuck you, I'm a Jew from Philly*, Gottlieb had taught his boys to think. *The city's already beaten me down in a thousand ways you can't imagine. Try to show me something I ain't seen.*

Here they were again, Gottlieb versus Hertzman for all the gelt. Hertzman was moonlighting this season in charge of the Visitations, a quotidian Brooklyn squad, usually nothing more than a pit stop on the way to playing the big boys. They traditionally had an aging, mostly Irish crew and a lack of imagination. But Hertzman had come in talking tough and installed his "system," scaring opposing coaches with his reputation and his dirty conjurer's tricks. The Visitations responded with a streak of questionable play unseen in the league since World War I. Fair was foul and foul was fair. They won a lot of games, even more than the SPHAs. So when it came time to determine the champion, once again Gottlieb had to pile the players into his hearse, have them sit in the bucket seats with their knees up to their ears, and make the slow, gas-powered crawl through the vile swamps of Jersey. *Oh, look*, the players thought as the skyline came into view, *we're almost in New York again*. And then they fell asleep.

For a team that played its games adjacent to (and drew its name from) a monastery, the Visitations didn't exactly give off an air of simplicity and peace. Their fans made the SPHA crowd look like ascetic pilgrims—when you pack two thousand Irishmen in the midst of their weekend benders into a bandbox firetrap, some of them are bound to stray. So the players would have a better chance of surviving the game intact, the team put up a ten-foot-high chicken wire fence around the court, with door-shaped holes cut into the wire at intervals. The wire had been in place for a while and was getting rusty. This created its own set of hazards if a player crashed the boards, missed, and went hurtling into a loose tine. Also, it was hard to play basketball effectively after getting a glass bottle smashed over your head.

Game time approached. As usual, Gottlieb had the motivation down, even though his team didn't need much. When you're sitting on splintery benches in a basement, the lights flickering like Frankenstein's laboratory, rusty water steadily dripping down, and scores of people directly above you roaring for your head, you can either lie down like dogs or stand and fight. The SPHAs always chose the latter. Gottlieb stood by the door, a big green exit sign over his head, and waved a newspaper in the air.

"The *Daily News* has been talkin' about us again," he said. "This guy Gallico wrote an editorial called 'Basketball: The Jewish Game'!"

"He got that right," Inky said, and the team laughed.

Gottlieb read from the piece aloud.

"'Curiously, above all others, the game appeals to the temperament of Jews. While a good Jewish basketball player is a rarity'"—Gottlieb had to stop there to make room for the curses that emerged from the mouths of his team, exactly like he'd planned—"'Jews flock to basketball by the thousands. It places a premium on the alert, scheming mind—flashy trickiness, artful dodging, and general smart-aleckness, traits naturally appealing to the Hebrew with his Oriental background.'"

"I ain't got an Oriental background," said Shikey Gothofer.

"I smoked opium once in Chicago," said Inky.

"I ate shrimp fried rice one time," Litwack said.

"My parents took me to see a lecture by Swami Vivekananda at the Self-Realization Fellowship in Boston," said Shostack.

That shut everyone up; Shostack had a way of really bringing down the room.

"So you see the problem here, boys," Gottlieb said. "Once again, they're underestimating us! Sure, we're alert, scheming, and tricky. Sometimes, when we have to be. But we're a lot more too. Are we tough?"

"Yeah!" went the team.

"Are we strong?"

"Yeah!"

"Are we fast?"

"Yeah!"

"Are we Jews?"

"Fuck yeah!"

"Now, this team we're gonna play tonight, they're run by one of us. Hertzman thinks he knows all our tricks, but he's got the wrong squad in mind if he thinks he can outcoach me. We're the best that ever was and ever will be. I truly believe that. They've been underestimating our people for two thousand years. Maybe not us specifically, and not in a basketball context, but I think you understand what I'm saying. We always win somehow. So tonight, no matter what happens, no matter how many times you get knocked down or hit in the balls, remember that you're Jews, and Jews always get up when it counts. Tonight we're gonna show Brooklyn how it's done."

That worked the boys up into a pretty good lather. These men weren't doing it for money or for women or even for the love of the game. Their drive ran deeper than that, and that was why they usually won. Gottlieb watched them strap on their knee pads and hip pads, and he felt proud, like Moses must have felt on the Mount when he first introduced the Ten Commandments. Of course, Moses didn't have to watch a bunch of hairy, sweaty guys drop aluminum cups into their shorts and adjust their balls, but the contemporary world presented unique challenges. *They would win tonight*, Gottlieb thought. *They'd better*. He'd hocked a hundred and fifty dollars' worth of watches so he could lay down a side bet with Hertzman. If the team lost, they'd be buying their own dinner tonight. But he didn't want to tell them that. It was a fine line between motivating guys and making them nervous. Gottlieb had been walking it for years.

"Gentlemen," Gottlieb said, "are you ready?"

They were.

"Then let's play some Jewball!"

• fourteen •

THROUGH THE fence, Inky could feel them spitting. Fat, wet, yellow-green Irish loogies rained down on him and on the rest of his teammates. It had started at the opening tip, and it hadn't let up at all. Gottlieb was screaming at the ref to make it stop, but the ref had no vested interest in angering the home crowd. Not for what he was getting paid.

The Visitations had been well trained in the art of inflicting minor, surreptitious pain on their opponents. Finger touched eye, elbow hit nose, knee pressed into groin. Less subtle actions went down as well. One thrown hip sent Fitch flying into the chicken wire, opening a two-inch gash along his arm. He had to go to the bench for that one, and he bit on a leather belt as Zink smeared his wound with a little Mercurochrome. But the joke was on the Visitations, because it wasn't his shooting arm.

After the initial shock passed and the Visitations scored a couple of quick buckets, before one of which Inky shamefully saw an assist go through his own legs, the SPHAs clamped down hard. Gottlieb knew who the weak ball handlers were and had the team ready to deploy a series of smothering traps. They swarmed. Litwack drained a set shot. Fitch headed toward the basket, Shostack slid in, and a Visitation hit him at an unhealthy speed. The poor guy hit the ground, blood pouring from his nose. Fitch moved in for an easy five-footer that Inky had looped around Shostack's left haunch. The other team started to act sad and disoriented. After Inky split a pair of free throws, the SPHAs were up 13–6, and things were looking good.

Hertzman had called time-out, which meant three minutes of Gottlieb ranting with his chalkboard. Inky half listened, half watched the opposing team's bench, which sat silently, as though a particularly strict schoolmarm had punished them. It didn't look like they were having very much fun. And then the crowd began to chant.

"Brennan! Brennan! Brennan!"

Seriously? Inky thought. *They want Brennan? He hasn't played in nearly a decade.* But then Hertzman stood up from the bench and started clapping, as though he were conducting, and his players stood as well.

"Brennan! Brennan! Brennan!"

The doors to the home locker opened, revealing a dark hallway. And then into the light stepped Joe Brennan, the pride of Prospect Park, six feet three inches of Irish basketball heaven. Brennan was the only legitimately good player the Visitations had ever produced. He'd played hard, he'd played clean, and he'd shot like a smooth dream.

Brennan looked ridiculous to Inky. His hair had gone almost completely white. There were wrinkles around his eyes and around his mouth. He had to be at least forty-five. But Hertzman wouldn't be bringing Brennan out if there weren't at least a little oil left in his joints. Gottlieb recognized this too, right away. He turned to Litwack.

"We're gonna play Harry's four-and-one," Gottlieb said. "But, Harry, you've got to guard that guy special. Brennan can score."

This would keep Litwack busy. He wouldn't be available for shooting. Inky would have to lead the way, which was how he liked to do things. Maybe now if Litwack was busy, people would see who the real star was, and—

"Watch it, Inky!" Shostack yelled. He dove low and slammed into Inky, dropping him to the floor. Inky thought Charlie had gone insane. But he didn't think that a couple of seconds later, as a twenty-pound sandbag hit the court and burst open, just like Inky's head would have done if the bag had connected. The crowd booed; Inky was still alive.

"Keep your head in the game, Lautman," Gottlieb said. "Or I'll make *you* guard Brennan."

The floor was soon covered in blood and sand. The detritus accumulated faster than the rag boys could clean. The old lady with the knitting needles was sitting in the front row like she always did, and she kept poking at the SPHAs as they ran by, which gave them pause before they dove for a save out of bounds. It looked like the circus had come to town and the lions had feasted. There'd be more of that in the next hour. The Visitations were a lot tougher with a real scorer on the floor.

Brennan made two tough shots with Litwack in his face and then stole the ball from Sundodger, who'd been seminapping on the court, and passed it downcourt for another easy one. Inky came back and drained a quick set shot off the dribble, but the Visitations responded. The next two minutes were a war of defensive attrition and sloppy ballhandling. It was 15–14 at the halftime buzzer. The SPHAs ran for the lockers with their arms covering their heads, but it wasn't enough. Some clown came at Inky and jammed a lit cigar into his thigh. Inky howled in pain and dismissed his assailant with a shot to the chops. Brooklyn didn't appreciate the value of a good cigar.

"I had to go shopping with my wife for undergarments the other day," Gottlieb was saying in the lockers. "Because she made me. And I looked around at the salesgirls and I thought, you know, I bet these ladies could play basketball a lot better than my pussy-ass team! Fuck on a stick, what is wrong with you boys? Do you wanna win, or do you just wanna pick your asses? Well? Do you? Do you?"

The SPHAs sat there and took it. Gottlieb screamed at them all the time. They knew what they needed to do to win the title; how they were going to get out of the arena alive was another matter, but they figured they'd just have to improvise. First they'd win; *then* they'd survive.

Maybe they should have paid attention. The Visitations came onto the court mean and ready. They made two shots within the first minute, and then Brennan picked Inky's pocket when Inky tried a mean crossover dribble. That was enough to get Gottlieb to scream for time, before they'd even broken a sweat. But he had to. They were already down five points. Any more and the game might get out of reach. The SPHAs took to the huddle ready to absorb a blizzard of invective. Instead, Gottlieb sat quietly. You could see the steam rising from his collar, but he kept it controlled.

"Do you want to win?" he said.

"Sure we want to win," Inky said. "We ain't in this for the pussy."

"That's enough lip, Lautman. I want you all to do what you have to do to win. Whatever you have to do. Got it?"

They said they did.

"I mean do *anything*," Gottlieb said. He put a big wad of tobacco in his mouth, not his usual vice, and began to chomp.

"Zink," he said, "gimme your hat."

Zinkoff complied. But when Gottlieb spit into his hat, he wished he hadn't.

"Don't say it," Gottlieb said to him. "I'll buy you a new one when we win."

The whistle blew. The muscle team took the court: Inky, Litwack, Shostack, Fitch, and Shikey. Litwack drained a shot immediately, and then they clamped down hard. Brennan wasn't going to be able to breathe. Every time he saw the ball, he got double-teamed. When he drove to the basket, a hard hip met his flank. No passing lane went unguarded. If a Visitation player even thought about grabbing an offensive rebound, he got an elbow to the teeth.

It was no easier on the other side, but the SPHAs were patient and scoring enough. Inky took a hard one to the jaw, but it didn't bring a whistle. Without stopping the action, Gottlieb screamed at Inky to go to the bench. Inky jogged backward. Gottlieb reached into his mouth. His hand was red and covered with slime. He dragged it across Inky's chin.

"Go show that to the ref," Gottlieb said.

Nice show, Inky thought.

"Hey!" he shouted in the ref's direction, his jaw dripping red tobacco juice. "That was a foul!"

The ref couldn't dispute blood, even fake blood. Inky got two shots and made them both. It was 28–27 SPHAs, with a little under seven minutes to go.

Brennan went on a relative tear, slipping the trap with some clever give-and-go action, hitting two shots. Then Litwack hit one, Inky stole one, and Inky made his shot. Shostack got a put-back, and suddenly the SPHAs found themselves up three. It was looking pretty good until Sundodger made the unforgivable mistake of fouling Brennan in the act, and the free throw tied it up at 34. Hertzman was tossing marbles onto the court in front of retreating Philly players. The crowd roared in desperation, longing to see the team they loved so much that it had moved to New Jersey and back *twice* in the last five years bring home a title that it didn't particularly deserve. It wasn't going to happen. Shostack was meat in the middle and the SPHAs swarmed with the four-and-one. From that point, the Visitations didn't get a chance to *take* a shot, much less miss. The SPHAs passed and cut, dribbled and waited, played their opponents like puppets, until finally Inky broke open, took an easy twelve-footer, and missed, only because a Visitation had lunged after him at the last possible second, catching his elbow and hurting his release. The shot hit the front rim, but the whistle blew with one second left. Inky had his chance to ice the title. Hertzman called time, thinking he might be able to play psychological games. Woe to the man who tries to put Dr. Freud on the couch. The schoolyard genius had made his fatal mistake. Gottlieb looked ready to burst out of his skin with joy.

The SPHAs huddled tight. Zink watched the perimeter for falling sandbags or bottles. The huddle emanated an almost unbearable stench; not everyone on the team bathed regularly anyway, and it had been a tough evening. The crowd yelled epithets mostly unheard since biblical times.

"You know what to do, Inky," Gottlieb said. "Like we talked about, right?"

"I got it," Inky said.

With that, Zinkoff rushed off the court and out the side door, which confused everyone but Gottlieb and Inky; clearly he was privy to whatever plan they'd concocted. The SPHAs took their positions around the key, Fitch and Litwack in position for the box out, a couple other guys in the backcourt in case of unimaginable disaster. Inky sent the first free throw through clean, and the guys on the bench started to celebrate. Gottlieb told them to sit down because the party had just begun. The second shot missed cold off the front of the rim, the ball shooting straight for Inky. He got it clean with his palm, scooped it, and it went through at the buzzer, never giving the Visitations a chance to touch the ball and sending the SPHAs to a three-point win when, really, one would have sufficed.

Inky turned to the crowd, gave a little bow, and then pulled down his shorts, revealing his full, circumcised glory. *Fuck you*, Inky mouthed. *Fuck you all.*

The SPHAs had about twenty seconds to get out of there before the crowd tore down the chicken wire. Gottlieb was already by the fire exit, screaming at the team to move, move, move! They could mail him the trophy. Right now, he had to get his guys out of there. He didn't really have the funds for a funeral.

Inky got to the car intact. They all did. Because Inky had agreed to show the crowd his schlong, Gottlieb had given him a fifty-dollar bonus and the promise that he'd get to ride shotgun. Meanwhile, Litwack sat in the backseat, uncelebrated. They peeled out of the alley, bottles shattering against the trunk and the back bumper. Inky thought, *This is why I play the game.*

· fifteen ·

THEY HAD a victory parade, though it wasn't exactly that because the city didn't give them permits and wouldn't help them advertise. Also, it rained. So basically Zinkoff drove the car around the block and then everyone went to a banquet room at the Broadwood and got drunk. Joe from the Bucket lent the use of his still. He'd decided to keep running it after Prohibition because his stuff tasted better. There was plenty of wine about, because Jews like wine, and also beer and other bottles the contents of which, by the time someone opened them, didn't really matter much. Everyone's grandma made their special kugel, Shostack's mother stewed a shit ton of brisket, and Zinkoff got his uncle to donate corned beef, sausages, and sauerkraut. Fitch had the band play, and everyone on the team danced around with the trophy. Shikey was spotted under the bleachers making out with someone else's wife.

Gottlieb, bloated and staggering, took the microphone. He blurted something that sounded like "Heshefaloo blurwallblodget," and then blubbered out Inky's name. Inky took the stand and said, "I done good, we done good, you all done good! Here's to Jewball!" He held up the trophy and everyone cheered. Then it was Litwack's turn and everyone settled in for the long march. It was assumed he'd run for office someday.

Litwack spoke of sacrifice and of perseverance in the face of adversity. He told tales of courage and hardship, of immigrant sacrifice and the toughness of Jews, while taking great care not to insult anyone else in the process. The SPHAs were about community, he said, and family and brotherhood and love. They were the very spirit and salt of Philadelphia, and he was proud to call them brothers.

Fucking Litwack.

The party ran deep into the night, and by the time Inky got on the trolley, the sun was already considering making an appearance. Natalya kept him company. They groped each other all the way home, staggered up the steps, and fell into a drunken death sleep, not finishing the deal until long after noon, when the bottles started breaking downstairs.

She put her head on his chest and looked at him with loving eyes.

"I've got a meeting tonight, Inky," she said.

"That's good," said Inky, distractedly.

Loving eyes quickly turned to frustration. Inky could see he'd said something wrong. But he never knew exactly what with this dame. *That's the cost*, he thought, *when you get to it with someone smarter than you.*

"Inky?"

"What."

"Stop ignoring me."

"I ain't ignoring you."

"Then why didn't you ask me about my meeting?"

"I don't know. I just didn't."

"Don't you care about it?"

"I can't care if I don't know."

"Well, maybe I shouldn't tell you."

"Please tell me. And also tell me what I did wrong."

"Only if you're interested."

"I'm interested, dammit! I'm really fucking interested."

"I'm just teasing, Inky. Jeez. It's the Jewish Students' Defense Coalition."

"Oh yeah?"

"Well, we're meeting tonight."

"So you said."

"I'd really like for you to come."

"I don't think so."

"Maybe you could speak to the group."

"I ain't much of a speaker."

"But they look up to you. And I want you to tell them what you saw at the Garden."

Fuckin' broads, Inky thought. *Never get involved. Don't even try.* But he felt something for this one, something deep-seated, like a common purpose, almost. That just killed him. She had him like a trained puppy.

"It's at the student center at seven thirty," she said.

"Fine," he said. "But I gotta see Gottlieb first."

"You do whatever you have to do, tough guy," she said.

She climbed on top of him like his crotch was a saddle. He still felt pretty worn down after the previous night. But the gates of Jerusalem had opened, and he was helpless to resist.

The players went to the JCC thinking they were just going to drop off their laundry and pick up their share of the winnings, but when they got there Gottlieb was sitting around looking somber and sweaty. He had an ice pack attached to the side of his face like he'd just gotten a tooth pulled; he'd been into the hooch harder than anyone the night before, and he was in no shape to recover quickly.

They all showed up at about the same time, because punctuality is one of the hallmarks of teamwork. Also because it was payday. Gottlieb had them all sit down. In a low voice, because that was about all he could muster, he told them the whole sad tale, of how he'd taken out a sure-thing gambling debt, about how that debt had gone sour, and about how now those Bund bastards wanted him to repay the debt by throwing a game in Minneapolis, which would take place about two months hence.

"Jesus Christ, Eddie," Litwack said. "That's a huge fucking mess."

"I know, I know," Gottlieb said, "and I'd curse my mother's grave if she would just go ahead and die already, but she won't die because she doesn't want me to have an extra room in my house or even one minute to myself ever again."

"Be that as it may," Litwack said, "we can't throw a game to the Bund. It's not in our nature."

"We ain't gonna throw no game to no one," said Inky. "We're tough and we know we're tough. We can beat anyone, and it shouldn't matter that Eddie was stupid with his money. I've seen what the Bund can do. And I sure as hell ain't gonna be the one to light the match."

"Very eloquent, Inky."

"Fuck you, Litwack."

"I'm serious. You're right. We need a plan. You got a plan, Eddie?"

"I was kind of planning to lose and then go home out of debt," Gottlieb said.

The players didn't like that. At all. In fact, they refused, and they determined that the Bund wouldn't have its day, even symbolically. Not on their watch.

"All right, then, smart guys," Eddie said. "There's another way."

As Gottlieb outlined his strategy for getting to Minnesota without losing what remained of his shirt, the team listened with quiet resolve. For Inky, it would be easy, just a couple of months more of playing basketball for money. He had no real overhead. But for some of the guys, it meant putting their jobs on hold, or for Shostack, it meant missing an audition or two, and then there were the families to consider. Even Inky found himself considering Natalya's needs, a sure sign he was sunk for her. But as Gottlieb sketched out the route, everyone liked what he saw. Eddie had been a major dope, but now they knew they had an opportunity for something good, something they wouldn't regret in the morning or in the mornings to come. A guy can't say that every day.

The practices would start tomorrow, Gottlieb said, and they'd be harder than ever. There was ball, and there was Jewball, and if they were gonna win, they'd better demonstrate the difference, with emphasis. Inky stood, took off his collared shirt, and in his undershirt, walked over, pulled a ball off the rack, gave a few dribbles, and drained a set shot from fifteen feet.

"We're gonna start this now," he said.

His teammates, with not a reluctant sigh among them, got up to join.

No one wanted to wait.

sixteen

THE JEWISH Students' Defense Coalition met in an appropri-ately dingy room in a run-down boardinghouse on the western edge of the Penn campus, close to Bund territory. To the students, the setting felt dangerous and appropriate. The dim light, cheap brown wallpaper, and almost deliberate paucity of seating gave the whole affair a patina of authenticity, as though any form of popular struggle didn't deserve bright colors and good sight lines. Revolt was best planned sitting cross-legged on the floor.

Inky arrived before seven thirty p.m.—he was always early for everything, and always had been, though he'd come to realize that didn't exactly make the things he did end any more quickly than they should—to find almost two dozen students filling the room with excited chatter. He noted that there was an equal number of men and women, which he found impressive. They looked like they read a lot; you could tell that they were serious of purpose, or at least wanted to be. The talk in the room was all Hitler, Hitler, Stalin, Franco, Hitler, midterms, and Mussolini, and a little Gertrude Stein thrown in—about what Inky would have expected, as though history were some crazy surrealist theatrical experiment being performed for these kids' benefit. Such was the folly and privilege of being young and bright in an epoch of seeming importance.

As soon as he entered, he saw her, looking sharp and beautiful in the cutest little beret. Natalya spotted Inky and gave him a warming smile. She signaled him over to join her conversation.

She was talking to a garrulous sort who looked like her brother Charlie gone to pot, or at least on the way there. The guy had a massive torso leading to a double-thick neck with veins that stuck out like rail ties and a big face—not fat, just big—from the eyebrows to the chin to the nose, to the cranium itself, which balanced there like a great sweaty, unshaven balloon. His collared shirt was open maybe one button too many, and his chest hair billowed forth like swamp grass. This was David Pritzker, a junior in the history department and the founding chairman of the JSDC. If nothing else, he knew how to hold the space.

"Comrade Pritzker," she said, "this is Inky Lautman, of the South Philadelphia Hebrew Association."

"I've seen him play," Pritzker said. "He's quite the passer."

"And he's my boyfriend," Natalya said, giving Inky's arm a charming little squeeze.

"A boyfriend, eh?" Pritzker said.

This made Inky uncomfortable. He'd never been anyone's boyfriend before. But he didn't correct her, and didn't want to, which meant it was probably true. Why else would he be here when he could instead be at home by himself watching the flies crawl up the wall or maybe down at the bar beating up deadbeats for money? It must be love.

"Inky," Natalya said, "David and I were together for a while last year, but we split."

"The reason she gave was semantical differences," Pritzker said. "Can you believe that, Inky?"

"I don't even know what those are," Inky said. "Sounds serious."

Pritzker roared, much too loudly. He slapped Inky on the back.

"I like this one, Natalya," he said.

Inky didn't like this guy much in return.

Pritzker took to the dais. He had a bottle in his left hand, and he swilled from it with great gusto.

"Welcome, my fellow Hebraic warriors!" he said. "I'm glad to see the vicissitudes of the day did not dampen your fighting spirit and that you're here despite your multiple commitments. We stand, as you know, at the crossroads of history. Great dangers surround us, and…"

What a blowhard, Inky thought. But the JSDC looked at him raptly, as though he had something to say. Inky couldn't help but wonder if the guy could take a punch. He decided that, yes, he could probably take about a half dozen in that gut of his before feeling it much. But he sure as hell wouldn't be able to dish one out.

"Our mission is clear: to provide a first line against the world-wide menace that knocks on our border and may even lurk next door. Traditional modes of rebellion might not work as well as they used to; we cannot resist passively or"—here went a swig of wine—"let those who might destroy us have safe harbor among our neighbors. The threat is clear, immediate, and pressing, and it's important to remember that the intellectuals, just like in Mother Russia, need to be the first line of defense against whatever is coming. Without our help, our brothers and sisters in the proletariat won't have the time or resources they need."

He got some applause for this.

"So now, the business at hand. As we talked about last week, we're considering changing our name. Some of you considered the Jewish Students' Defense Coalition too elitist. I personally think it's perfect, since it describes what we actually *are*, but this is a democratic body, and…"

And they were off, Inky thought, *talking and never doing anything*. This was why he'd always hated school. He did his learning with his hands and his fists, on the court, off the court, and everywhere in between. Maybe he didn't learn a lot, but he learned it the hard way, and permanently.

The JSDC considered a number of different names, including the League of Young Jewish Warriors, the People's Coalition for Jewish Defense, the Association of Young Jewish People Fighting Alongside Each Other for Justice, the Jewish Freedom Collective, various names with Hebrew words that Inky didn't understand because he'd been lax since his bar mitzvah, and Jews with Guns, rejected quickly and emphatically because it might call attention and because guns had been somewhat hard to come by since Prohibition had ended.

In the end, the suggestions came to a vote and everyone decided to stick with the original name because it meant something. What it meant, Inky wasn't sure. The meeting continued and the JSDC formed some committees and then they disbanded one of them because they realized that it contradicted the mission of another committee. Pritzker passed a bottle around and they all drank. The conversation grew merry and boisterous.

"Is there any more business before we adjourn to the campus for drinks and dancing?" Pritzker asked.

Inky raised his hand. "Yeah, I got something," he said.

"Ladies and gentlemen," said Pritzker, "we have a genuine Jewish hero in the room—or at least a basketball player. Mr. Lautman, you have the floor."

"I just wanted to know why you all don't do anything," Inky said.

"Pardon?" Pritzker asked.

"Inky, no," said Natalya.

"I mean, you seem to talk and talk about defending Jews, but all I really see are a bunch of kids getting drunk. Not that I have anything against getting drunk. I get drunk all the time. But at least I do something with the rest of my time. Look, you say you all want to fight the Bund. Well, I *have* fought the Bund. I've even worked for the Bund."

"A fifth columnist?" Pritzker said. "*Really?*"

"Yeah, really. They're a hard group, tough and stupid, and they've got money and the biggest fucking army in the history of the world at their backs. Let me tell you, they'd eat your bunch for afternoon tea. This ain't a group. It's a farce."

"You bastard!" Natalya said.

She slapped Inky hard across the face.

"I invited you here. These are my friends. And you treat them like this?"

Natalya turned and dashed from the room before Inky could get a thought out. He had no choice but to follow her. There was a lot of wine in her system. And his. If he played it right, he still might be able to get laid tonight. If he played it wrong, it might be years before he had sex again without paying.

Pritzker raised an eyebrow.

"It appears that the savior of the Jewish people has pressing romantic concerns," he said. "This calls for a drink!"

Not too many minutes earlier, Kunze and the count were playing chess nearby, listening to Wagner, drinking a little sherry, and generally having a lovely evening away from the weighty struggle for Aryan dominion over the earth. They talked openly about their favorite boyhood meals, the sporting scene, women (though not at length on that last topic, as neither had much recent experience), and inevitably, the Jewish question. For though this was their ostensible evening away from such conversation, the Jews just kept coming to mind.

It had been a hard few months for the Bund. The rally at the Garden had been a massive public relations disaster. Reaction to newsreel footage of the rally indicated that Americans liked their fascism a little more down-home and cornpone. The counter-insurgency began. New York's finest cracked down locally in the subsequent weeks. They liked to be the ones wielding the batons. Any possibilities of rebellion coming out of the boroughs got tamped down pretty quick. Meanwhile, the money had withered when the feds slapped Kuhn with a mighty tax lien. Most of the attorneys who knew how to handle such problems were, ironically if not surprisingly, Jewish, so Kuhn found himself with slim recourse.

This left the Pennsylvania chapter able to keep its headquarters open thanks only to the kind ministrations of the count's printing shop. Demand for anti-Semitic pamphletry still ran high in Germantown. But other initiatives had to be back-burnered. Even though they had many friends in the police department, these days the press was on the lookout for Hitlerian sympathy. On the East Coast, at least, the Bund now had to operate in the shadows.

But there still remained the basketball question. Gottlieb owed them a debt, point-blank. It might be hard to enforce legally, but a quick mention to the press would be enough to discredit Gottlieb and possibly the entire league. Kunze knew that, but he also knew that Gottlieb's botched arson of a few months previous, and the disturbing rumors from Kunze's spies in South Philly that the SPHAs were practicing harder than ever, meant that Gottlieb wasn't about to roll over and play dead.

"I wish Inky were still on our payroll," said Kunze.

"We overpaid," said Count von Lilienfeld-Toal as he stealthily slid a bishop across the board. "When you bring a cow to watch the slaughter, you might want to make sure that you kill it as well. And now it appears that our Mr. Lautman has found religion."

"We have other sources, other methods."

"But none so strong and punctual."

"True enough."

Inky had gimped half of Kunze's muscle and brained the other half, and they had yet to procure adequate replacements. Even in a community full of Bund sympathizers, it was hard to find people who sympathized to the extent that they'd break bones for pay.

"I guess the central question," said the count, "is what to do now."

"About what?"

"About this stupid game you've locked Gottlieb's men into. You don't actually think your little coterie of Teutonic giants is going to beat these Jewish devils, do you?"

"It could happen."

"Anything *could* happen, Kunze. But that doesn't mean anything will. If you lose this one, the press will destroy you. And you don't want to be Custer at the Bund's Last Stand. The führer will not be pleased if things don't go our way in Minneapolis."

Fuck the führer, Kunze thought, immediately glad that he didn't say it out loud. *I can do this my own way and do it right.*

"Well then," he said, "we'll just have to make sure they *do* go our way."

"You can fix the game any way you want," said the count. "I've seen these gentlemen play their sneaky game of hoops. They *invented* the game. They'll find a way to beat you."

"We know Gottlieb's not going to fly his boys out. That's a long drive. Maybe we make sure they never get to the game at all."

"That's very risky."

"We're at war," said Kunze, "or at least we will be soon. The killing has to start sometime."

"Of course it does."

"Now I just need to get a guy on the inside, someone with a beef against the SPHAs, who can get us a copy of their route."

"Such delusions," said the count as he moved his rook in for the finish.

After Kunze got his pocket picked by the count on the chessboard, he went for a little stroll on the Penn campus. He had sympathizers in the dorms. He knew that Jewish students' group would be meeting there tonight, and he wanted to keep tabs. Inky Lautman burst out of a lecture hall, chasing after a girl. This, Kunze hadn't expected. It seemed that an opportunity had just presented itself. He decided to follow at a reasonable distance.

A few yards away, Lautman caught the girl. Kunze hid behind a tree. He couldn't make out what they were saying, but she seemed upset. Lautman may have moved smoothly on the court, but he was no smooth talker, and he obviously wasn't winning her over. Inky reached to comfort her. She started to walk away. Inky moved to follow, then thought better and turned around dejectedly, walking back in the other direction. Kunze decided to risk confronting him. He stepped out from behind the tree.

"Women," he said.

"What the fuck are you doing here, Kunze?" said Inky.

"Just out for my evening constitutional."

"I thought you didn't believe in the Constitution."

"Those are different—Never mind, Inky. I could also ask what *you're* doing here."

"I came for a dame, what does it look like?"

"It looks like you didn't leave with what you came for."

"Ain't that the truth? And I had to deal with her ex-boyfriend. Some fat drunk baboon named Pritzker."

These were the typical personal follies of young people in love, Kunze thought. They played off one another as though their romantic choices really mattered in the face of history's mighty sweep. Kunze saw openings here, possibilities. His long relationship with Inky was finally bearing low-hanging fruit.

"Despite our many differences, Inky," Kunze said, "you're always welcome back on the payroll. Keeping in mind that our pay scale has declined slightly due to fiscal troubles."

"I don't want your dirty money," Inky said.

He moved as if to punch Kunze in the face. Kunze flinched and whimpered a little. And then Inky drew back.

"You know what?" he said. "Not tonight. I got bigger problems."

With that, Inky Lautman walked away into the slush. *I'm not sure that you* do *have bigger problems, Lautman*, thought Kunze. *And even if that's the case, I plan to make your problems a lot worse.*

Kunze turned back to his original route. Bedtime was approaching on sorority row, and he had big plans. He walked past the lecture hall again. A Falstaffian figure staggered out the door, holding a bottle of wine and singing "The Internationale" far too loudly. This guy didn't look like a child of starvation in any way. Suddenly, Kunze knew exactly where his plans were headed. He ran up to the guy.

"Pritzker?" he said.

"Is there a problem, Ossifer?" Pritzker said, holding up his bottle. "This is purely ceremonial. I was tasting it for the Sabbath."

"No problem at all, and do I look like police?" said Kunze.

"I don't know. I can't see particularly well at the moment. Too much ceremony, you see."

Pritzker staggered a bit. Kunze caught him by the arm.

"Do you happen to know someone named Inky Lautman?"

"I just met the man. Can't say I'm all that fond of him, though. He has a certain"—and here Pritzker hiccupped obnoxiously— "*relationship* with a friend of mine. Why do you ask?"

"Personal interest. My name is Kunze. And I have a proposition for you."

• s e v e n t e e n •

INKY WOKE in a strange room, facedown on a green velvet pillow, the air around him an amber swirl. Table lamps gave off a bluish light that had grown pale in the last hour, accented by the thin grayness of dawn that seemed to be just peeking under and around the blackout shades. Next to Inky, Shostack snored obliviously and happily. Where was he, and why was he there with Shostack?

A lone black woman perused the racing form at a long table, squinting through the blue-tinted dawn. Two other black guys, shoes off, wearing porkpie hats and white shirts open at the collars, passed a mouthpiece (connected to the most ornate hookah Inky had ever seen—part of it seemed to contain the figure of an elephant-headed man carved from ivory) back and forth across a couch, blowing great billows of sweet-smelling smoke. They sat directly across from Inky. One of them noticed that Inky's eyes had opened. He tipped his hat.

"Hell of a game last night, my friend," he said.

Inky nodded thanks. But last night's game wasn't registering in the forefront of his consciousness. His brain felt like a radio station tuned just to the right of the proper position on the dial. He still hadn't quite gained the coordinates. Meanwhile, from the actual radio, or maybe a hidden phonograph, came a weird and scratchy tune that gave the air in the room a simultaneous feeling of comfort and menace.

Dream about a reefer five feet long
Mighty Mezz but not too strong
You'll be high, but not for long
If you're a viper

I'm the king of everything
Well I gotta be high before I can swing
Light a tea and let it be
If you're a viper

Now when your throat get dry
And you know you're high
Everything is dandy
Truck on down to your candy store
Bust your conk on peppermint candy

Then you'll know your body's sent
You don't give a damn about payin' no rent
The sky is high and so am I
Whoa ho, if you're a viper

Harlem, Inky thought. Of course. He was definitely in Harlem.

In the history of basketball, there had really only been three teams that mattered: the Original Celtics (whose heyday was now in the past), the SPHAs, and then there was the all-Negro New York Renaissance. The Rens played every day, and twice on Sunday, and practiced when they weren't playing. No team passed the ball better (except maybe the SPHAs), and no team's defense was more aggressive or more coordinated. The Rens tried harder and jumped higher. One season, when they weren't affiliated with a league, they played 120 games and won 112, including, at one point, 88 in a row.

They had a lot in common with the SPHAs. Both staged their home games in ballrooms—the Rens occupied prime real estate on the second floor of Harlem's Renaissance Casino. Both were run by now-overweight, charismatic former stars—the Rens had the great Bob Douglas, who'd been putting together amateur contests as long as Gottlieb had. And they both knew what it was like to get into racially motivated brawls after games, though at least the SPHAs could usually get a hotel room on the way home and didn't need to use separate drinking fountains on Southern barnstorming tours.

Every Ren could tell a story about how, while the Rens were perusing the menu at a diner, a man would go behind the counter, grab a rifle off the wall, point it at them, and say, "Get out of here." They had no choice but to leave; they probably had another game soon, anyway.

Gottlieb and Douglas were great friends, and Gottlieb would often invite Douglas out for drinks but could never get him to do it. "The places you take me, I'm not welcome," Douglas said one time. "I don't need to face the icy stares of racist white men."

"You're not with white men now," Gottlieb said. "You're with Jews!"

Douglas laughed and agreed to join him. But they ended up going out in Harlem instead. It was a lot more fun up there.

Gottlieb always took the team to Harlem when he needed dough. He and Douglas had staged many epic, if low-scoring, affairs; Gottlieb, perpetually put upon in his own mind, thought Douglas got all the credit. When the Rens won, the games counted, and the SPHAs always seemed to come in for an exhibition contest at the end. The season the Rens took 112, they had a chance at 113 and were cocky enough to take on the SPHAs in Philly. They left three-point losers but still got called the champs because "the game didn't count." Well, it counted to Gottlieb, a hell of a lot, so he got them two games on the regular docket for the following season, both of which the SPHAs lost. Only one time had the SPHAs ever beaten the Rens in a game that had statistical meaning, and that was because Pop Gates sprained his knee with five minutes left and refused to come off the floor.

This time, though, would be different. Gottlieb was gearing the SPHAs up for the game of their life; there was no way they'd *ever* lose to the German team in Minnesota, but they didn't want to even make it close. And the best way to warm up would be a three-game away set against the Rens. The fact that Gottlieb could easily end up pocketing a few grand from the weekend was no small motivation, either. So they booked three nights at the casino, including a Friday night against Sabbath tradition, because that was a big night in Harlem. The boys could watch their mothers light the candles some other time. Ten thousand Negro basketball fans would attend their only shul that Friday. Most of them would be staying to see Count Basie play after the game.

The papers got excited, per their tendency, for the three-game set-to. One article (in a decidedly unprogressive rag) spread the idea that the game would be "a contest between the shifty-eyed Yids, with their outstanding lizard-like court vision, and the Niggers with their jungle-like speed, agility, and overall athletic ability. On the court, these two mysterious races will be almost evenly matched." The article may have been wrong on most counts, but neither Gottlieb nor Douglas minded. They'd been called much worse, and press was press.

For the first game, a Thursday-night affair that preceded an epic "stomp-off" between two jazz orchestras that went until five a.m., the Rens clearly had not been informed about the existence of Charlie Shostack. That's because he didn't often play against the smaller teams during the games the Rens had scouted. Shostack was a specialty weapon. The Rens had their own slab of pastrami in the middle—an agile All-Pro type with the singularly delightful name of Tarzan Cooper, who gave teams fits with his standing hook shot and passing out of the post. Shostack may not have been faster than Tarzan, but he was bigger. He had Tarzan muddled all night, getting in the way of his shots and forming an impenetrable concrete rebounding wall. On one play, Shostack set a hard but legal screen while Inky rolled toward the bucket. Cooper ran into Shostack and went down like Max Schmeling. He stayed down a while too, until the team doctor determined that Tarzan's shoulder had remained socketed.

With the middle neutralized, Gottlieb had his wings pick away at the perimeter. Litwack had been working on passing out of the double-team, and that left Inky open. This was one of those games where Inky couldn't miss, hitting all eight of his shots and all five of his free throws. Litwack shot six for ten, and Sundodger came down with some key rebounds. The SPHAs won 41–29. By the standards of their other games against the Rens, this marked an absolute rout. It left them feeling puffed.

Douglas knew this, and he also knew that Gottlieb could act the sore winner, especially if he was a perceived underdog. In the locker room after the game, Douglas told the Rens to treat the SPHAs liked honored guests—and to be sure to get them as shit-faced as possible. It would be seen as gracious hosting, but in Douglas's mind, it was just advanced game strategy. He knew that

Gottlieb didn't have the willpower to resist a night of debauchery and that neither did any of his boys except Litwack, but Litwack couldn't beat the Rens by himself.

Inky and the boys drank whiskey and stomped until about midnight, at which point they started getting too shaky to execute a proper dance step. One of the Rens pulled Inky and Shostack aside and said, "You gentlemen look tired. How'd you like to visit one of our famous tea pads?"

"I don't drink tea," Shostack said.

But Inky knew what the guy was talking about. He wanted to try the local wares. Shostack tagged along.

Weed had come to Harlem courtesy of a white man, a jazz musician named Mezzrow from whom the slang term "Mighty Mezz," meaning excellent marijuana, had derived. Mezz was good enough to qualify for various traveling orchestras, and during a swing through the Southwest, he developed a talent for identifying potent strains of Mexican cannabis and developed a rock-solid source that he wouldn't reveal to anyone. Mezzrow sold weed only to acquaintances (of which, admittedly, he had many), mostly sold it for the purchase price, and never sold it to kids. Because for many years he was the only source of quality weed in the neighborhood, the marijuana culture in Harlem took on a friendly, almost genteel quality; unlike the opium dens, where gambling and stabbing were common activities, in the "tea rooms," people mostly talked and listened to records.

The Ren players took Inky and Shostack to the basement door of a building on 136th Street. Various passwords were exchanged, and then they went through into a dank tunnel that smelled of rat droppings and something worse and unspeakable. This led them to another basement door and then a walk through several damp rooms full of rotting wood and two more doors before they finally reached something that looked habitable—a nicely painted door with red velvet padding around the edges.

"I feel like we walked three blocks underground," Inky said.

"You did," said the Ren.

The place was known as Kaiser's, and it was almost uncommonly clean, with nice couches and classic black-and-white decorative touches. Tuxedo-clad waiters walked the room with glasses of water and trays loaded with sweet-smelling joints. There didn't seem to be any alcohol around. A jukebox played the latest hits, as well as songs that Inky had never heard before. The air was filled with cool smoke and convivial laughter. Kaselman was already there, a sweet black babe on each arm. The ladies liked him because he stayed alert late, didn't get too grabby, and always picked up the tab. Inky and Shostack's hosts sat them down in a booth and ordered up a platter of Harlem's finest.

"Just relax," one of them said.

Inky had a few puffs and then a few more. He felt tingling in his forearms and in his throat. This Harlem shit was *strong*.

A broad sidled up next to him, saying, "Tell me, are you familiar with the poetry of Langston Hughes?" Inky couldn't say what that was, even. Shostack said, "I most certainly am." Inky heard a trumpet playing somewhere and then his head nodded.

He looked up, who knows how much later. Shostack and the poetry dame were rubbing heads together and laughing. One of Inky's hosts was talking.

"How ya doin', Lautman?" he said.

"Dizzy," Inky said.

"Yeah, that's about right."

"I think I need to get out of here. Go somewhere else. Find that trumpet."

"There ain't no trumpet," said the Ren. "Just the sweet melody of Mighty Mezz in your brain."

There was a trumpet. Inky could *prove* it. Just not right now.

"Shostack," he said, "we gotta go."

Shostack had his schnozz buried in the black girl's hair and didn't seem to be in a hurry.

"But LaVerne here and I were just analyzing the work of Jean Toomer," he said. "She says his romantic agrarianism is deliberately naive. I'm not so sure."

"What?" Inky said.

"We're discussing important things," Shostack said.

"Bring her along," said Inky. "Because we're leaving."

Back through the basement corridors they wandered. At some point, Inky's hosts said, "We got one other place we want to take you." Shostack was claiming to be in love with his poetry companion and he really wanted to go.

"No," Inky said. "My mouth is dry."

"We've got to wet it!" said one of the Rens.

The next few minutes moved by in a flicker. Inky's legs felt heavy. Cars drove past, but he saw them as if on a delay. His brain didn't match his eyes. They took him to a place called Chappy's, on the first floor of a 140th Street tenement.

"This one is for the late-nighters only," they said.

More blue light tinged the haze. Dancers stomped around the room, keeping their own time. Inky nursed a whiskey and wondered if he was, somehow, seeing the end of the world. Where was Shostack? What had happened to that dame? Oh, there they were, canoodling in the corner—or was it them? Did he still have his wallet? Yes, he did. And it still felt fat. One of the Rens brought him another glass, but why? And then it occurred to him that they were trying to get him drunk. By then it was too late to stop the process.

"I got a fat taste of somethin' good for you," said one of Inky's new friends.

Inky smoked some more. Next thing he could remember, he woke up next to Shostack in that dump at dawn, feeling like zoo animals had trampled him. The two Rens, across the room, acknowledged Inky with a wink. They'd done their job well.

The Rens slapped the SPHAs around pretty hard on night two. Just about the whole team was hungover except the sharp-as-always Litwack, and it showed in the box score. Shostack could barely walk. Tarzan turned him into a statue. He was just a slab of meat out there, a man with no aggression and no instinct. Inky fared somewhat better, though by the second half he was a little dizzy and losing a disturbing amount of sour-smelling sweat. The Rens' inside-outside game proved too much for him. They seemed to clog every passing lane.

With three minutes to go, when the outcome seemed certain, the Rens started passing the ball around with ridiculous efficiency. The SPHAs chased them around hopelessly, like puppies playing catch. The crowd in the ballroom went wild, like they'd gotten to witness an encore before the end of the concert. They loved it when the Rens played keep-away. Gottlieb fumed on the sidelines, yelling at the refs:

"HEY! They're showin' off! That's illegal! Wake up, you sheep fuckers!" That got him a technical foul and one more point for the home team. The Rens won 35–26.

Gottlieb saved the height of his wrath for the lockers. It smelled like blood and vomit. A foul blanket of stale *schvitz* hung over the defeated room. "You guys played like a bunch of winos out there!" Gottlieb shouted. "I'm paying you to be athletes, not barflies."

The SPHAs hung their heads, except for Litwack, who filed his nails because he knew that the guilt didn't fall on him, as usual. He'd gone to bed early after reading a magazine.

"Let me ask you," Gottlieb said. "What were you doing last night?"

No one said a thing.

"Well, I know, because I got spies. Lautman, Shostack, you let those goddamn shines take you to a reefer den. Now, I got nothing against reefer. I don't even know what it is. Except that it smells like shit and it can't be good for you, the way you looked out there."

Gottlieb paced. He liked to do that, because a coach needed to bring drama and fear into the equation. He was dealing with men half his age and twice as strong, and he had to keep control.

"The night before a game!" he said. "Ain't you got any goddamn sense, Lautman?"

"Sorry, Eddie," Inky said. "It was fun."

"And the music was good," Shostack added.

"This isn't about fun!" Gottlieb yelled. "This is basketball, you fucks! But if you behave like boys, I'll treat you like boys. As soon as I'm done flapping my gums here, you all are going back to the hotel. You're going to eat in the hotel restaurant. Dinner and breakfast and everything else. In between, you're in your rooms, doors bolted. And you're not allowed to leave until we go to practice at ten a.m. You give me something good there, and *maybe* I'll let you go out for lunch. Got it?"

They got it. Eddie had shamed them enough. And they knew that, thus far, these hadn't been classic games. The press wasn't buzzing enough. Exhibitions weren't worth the public's while. The rivalry between the Rens and the SPHAs was too tame, with too much respect. Fans wanted warriors, not good-time Charlies flicking the ball around like girls playing badminton.

There couldn't be any more parlor tricks. The SPHAs had pride, and they felt the wounds. They weren't less than people said; they were more, and they had to show their best.

Game three would tell the true tale.

After a better-than-decent practice the next day, Gottlieb's rage subsided. He went into avuncular mode, taking the team down to the Garment District to collect some fancy new double-breasted plaid mackinaws that he'd bought for them, with warm-up jackets to go over. They almost squealed with delight, like he'd asked them to go steady, and the new duds gave them some juice. That night they ran onto the court looking sharp and feeling loose; no Harlem team was going to outflash them. They danced around the basket doing passing and set-shot drills. Right before the game started, they dropped their outer layers to reveal the team initials samekh, pe, he, and aleph, all folded into a Jewish star. The SPHAs had woken up sober, and they'd worked hard all day. Their pride had returned.

It was a battle from the beginning. Shostack gave Tarzan Cooper fits, like he had in the first game, but Cooper used moves on Shostack at the other end, drawing double-teams and leaving shooters open on the wings. Size, as it often did, canceled itself out, leaving the game to be won or lost outside the paint. Everyone dove for every ball. Zach Clayton, a guy from Philly who would have taken a spot on the SPHAs if he'd been white, made a shot, under pressure, from his *knees*. Even Sundodger showed some passion, poking a guy in the eye after he'd been poked himself. Inky made both the shots the Rens had given him, and the one free throw, but points were a rarer commodity than a virgin on Purim. The Rens held a slip of a lead, 17–15, at halftime, but they sure hadn't cornered the market on bruises or hustle. The SPHAs went to the lockers feeling good and knowing they had a hell of a chance.

They sat in silence, staring at the floor. That was when Gottlieb knew they were going to carry the day. Once again, the sense of constant put-uponness and inchoate martyrdom—which he'd worked so hard to instill in his team—had risen to the surface, and that meant victory. Gottlieb went to take a leak and a slug of whiskey from his silver flask. When he came back, they were still sitting, no pacing around, not even a leg twitch, almost like store mannequins, almost creepy. The SPHAs came back onto the court stoically, single file, while the Rens walked around the lower levels of the stands, hugging their mothers and glad-handing their political representatives. Home court had its advantages but could also make you soft if you weren't paying attention. Gottlieb wondered if the Rens had even gone in for halftime. Meanwhile, the SPHAs bloodlessly took a five-minute warm-up and prepared to knock the crap out of their friends from Harlem.

The SPHAs scored three baskets almost before the Rens had their warm-ups off. Finally, the other team woke up and got down to business, jostling inside, making long set shots from the perimeter, restoring order. It was 26–21 after Shostack split a couple of free throws, 26–23 a few seconds after that, and then they went back and forth for a while until Inky spotted an opening, swiped the ball from the Ren point guard, and drove down for a six-foot spot-on setter that drained the nylon out of the net and drained the life from the crowd. They'd gone to 36–31 with twenty seconds to go. It looked like the SPHAs were going to (yet again unofficially) claim the title of the best basketball team in the known universe.

They had the ball. Fitch got an easy, wide-open shot that looked like it was headed straight down. The glass backboard moved. Inky looked up. It was attached to cables from the balcony. A couple of fans were up there, pulling on them. Litwack got the rebound, posted up, turned around, and shot. Again, the backboard moved. Inky screamed at the refs, who ignored him. Gottlieb screamed at the refs, who gave him a technical. The Rens made the shot and were only down by four. Then they had the ball and made another. Inky got the shooter on the arm, the shooter made his free throws, and the SPHAs' lead was one.

Inky looked toward the bench. Gottlieb was clutching his chest and gasping for air. The man had no business working in such a pressure-packed job. Inky, on the other hand, could handle the gig. Sundodger got him the inbounds, and he dribbled to his right after feinting to his left. The Rens wanted to foul him because they knew the backboard would move and the refs wouldn't do a thing, so he had to evade them completely. *The key*, Inky thought, *would be to stay low to the floor, as parallel as possible, and to maintain control, moving the ball from one hand to the other*. This game had everything to do with balance. The Rens couldn't catch him. They didn't even come close. Inky ran like a rat that had found the cheese. The SPHAs won by one point.

At least this wasn't one of those arenas where they had to flee as soon as the game was over. The other team shook their hands.

"Congratulations, you little Jew bastard," one of the Rens said. Inky thanked him. He took it as a compliment.

Meanwhile, Gottlieb appeared to have regained control of his heart for the moment. He gave Inky a big hug. Gottlieb smelled like a hospital.

"You are one sneaky fucker, Lautman," he said.

"I learned it all from you, Eddie," said Inky. "I thought you were gonna die back there."

"Not tonight, Lautman."

"I wouldn't have minded."

"You would have if Litwack had taken over the team, like it says in my will."

"Fucking Litwack."

"You wanna show me where this tea room is, or what?"

And so it came to pass that Inky and Gottlieb got stoned together. Inky went back to the hotel at about two a.m., leaving Gottlieb in the hands of a couple of lady poets they'd met on the couches. Inky wasn't interested. He still felt sore about the breakup with Natalya and thought about her more than he should have. That girl hurt his heart. He wanted to call or write, but he knew he couldn't. So instead he went to bed.

Gottlieb never said exactly what happened to him that night. But he showed up at the team car at ten a.m. looking more satisfied than Inky'd ever seen him. It was a long and happy ride to Wilkes-Barre.

· eighteen ·

NATALYA SHOSTACK sat in the University of Pennsylvania library, writing Inky Lautman's name over and over again in the margins of her Theory of Education class notebook. John Childs called for a definition of democracy that included economic justice and equality of opportunity. Inky, Inky, Inky, always Inky and forever. *Damn him*, Natalya thought. Her parents had raised her to believe that she was better than any man and subservient to none. And then comes this rough-hewn jock living above a *bar*, for Ben Gurion's sake, who has no political principles to speak of, and who beats people up on the side for money. Natalya may have had a tender soul for social justice, but she also had a pragmatic heart. She always figured that maybe she'd marry one day, an equal with an equal number of degrees or an equal passion for breaking the chains in which ordinary people everywhere were held. But the cause, whatever that might be, would come first. Inky, with his shrugs and his gruff dismissals of the life of the mind, didn't fit into her schematic in any way. He threw around his ignorance like a chimp flinging feces. And yet there he stood, smug and broad shouldered, at the front of her imagination.

From behind, she heard, "Natalya Shostack. In the library. And it's not even midterms. Fortune smiles."

"What do you want, David?"

She turned to look. David Pritzker wore a ridiculous brown leather cap lined with fake fur. It made him look like a guard at a Siberian insane asylum. He had a stack of books in his arms, which he plopped on the table far more loudly than he should have. If given a choice between a million dollars and entering a room quietly, David would have ended up in debtor's prison.

"What I *want* and what I *do* are two completely different things," he said. "I needed some books, and this is where you come."

Pritzker leaned in. Natalya smelled wine on his breath.

"Still not over your sports legend, I see," he said. "It's hard to let someone go when they sweat all the time."

She snapped the notebook closed.

"Hmph," she said. "I'd be happy if I never saw that third-rate malcontent again in my life."

"Don't know why you'd feel that way. He's not such a bad sort."

"He's crude and obnoxious and he disrupted our meeting."

"Eh," Pritzker said, waving his hand. "That meeting was boring, anyway. Lautman was just saying what we all thought. Come on, admit it, you'd rather be with him right now than doing some boring homework."

"I would not!"

"Right."

He ran a finger through her hair.

"Then maybe you'd want to resume where we left off."

She swatted him away.

"That would be even worse."

"Typical Natalya. Leading a horse to water."

"I'm not *leading* you anywhere, David. Isn't it just possible that a girl can live her life? That she can determine on her own what to do?"

"Sure it is, sweetheart," David said. "You know that's how I feel. You don't need to follow me or Lautman or any man. Where is Inky, anyway?"

"Why do you want to know?"

"Because I'm a fan. They're on tour and I like to keep tabs."

"Well, last I heard, the team is playing tonight in Scranton and then driving to Pittsburgh. Overnight. After a game. To save money on hotel rooms."

"Did you say Scranton to Pittsburgh?"

"Yes. Who would want to go on that trip? What dreadful country."

"I have some friends in Pittsburgh who might want to see the great SPHAs play."

"Friends in Pittsburgh?" Natalya said. "Impressive."

"Are they taking the main road?"

"I would imagine so."

"Good. That's good."

David's behavior had been so odd that Natalya kept thinking about it all afternoon and on into the evening, through dinner, barely touching her brisket. David usually talked glibly, sometimes for hours, but never acted. He never did anything. The only time he stopped talking was to write, during which time he'd hole himself up until he'd produced an adequately bombastic left-wing screed. Occasionally, if he were up to no good, he'd revert to the old blubber-and-bumble.

In the library, David had behaved like he had nasty plans, and Natalya thought they might involve Inky. She didn't think they were about her. Though she was sure that David would welcome her back, he didn't lack for other female interest; besides, possession, of any sort, wasn't his style. Whatever scheme he was stirring had nothing to do with romantic jealousy, at least not directly.

When David had said he didn't mind how Inky had behaved at the meeting, Natalya didn't believe him. Inky had shown him up; David's fragile ego couldn't take too many shocks. She was almost as sure that she'd made a mistake in the library by letting the SPHAs' tour route slip. By the time she'd pulled together the puzzle, or at least as much of it as she could assemble, it was after nine p.m., and she was back at her parents' house. Outside, the rain came down with intent to hurt. Something big was about to go down. She had to warn Inky.

"Daddy?" she said, putting on her best little girl voice. "Can I please use the phone?"

Her father put down the volume of Woodrow Wilson's speeches that he used whenever he wanted to fall asleep early.

"What for?"

"Private business," she said. "I need to make some long-distance calls."

Pa Shostack sucked his meerschaum. Natalya shuffled. Every minute he spent obfuscating counted.

"All right," he said. "But you'll have to pay any charges more than a dollar."

That seemed like a deal.

Making sure that no one was around to hear, Natalya requested an operator in Scranton, Pennsylvania. When she got one, she asked about local hotels. There were quite a few. She got connected to one that told her Jews weren't welcome. The second call didn't go much better. The third place she tried, the desk clerk told her that the SPHAs had stayed there last night, but that the team bus had pulled out of the lot about twenty minutes before.

Natalya's instincts had been right, but her timing had been lousy. She felt concerned, though not anywhere close to uncontrollably worried. Inky was a big boy. They all were. Bigger than most. She just hoped they were big enough to handle whatever was coming their way.

Puffing all the way, David Pritzker ran straight back to his boardinghouse from the library. He had the information they wanted. Initially, he'd refused when he found out they were from the Bund. They'd given him a little cash. Still, he'd refused. They made it clear that they'd break his legs if he didn't cooperate. Thus Pritzker had made his collaborationist bed, and now he was tossing in the sheets. *Never enter a deal with fascists while you're drunk*, he noted to himself. *They'll nag you to your grave.*

He had Kunze on the line.

"I got what you wanted," Pritzker said.

"We can't talk on the phone," said Kunze. "Someone may be listening."

"Then I'll come to your office."

"No. Be in Fairmount Park in forty-five minutes."

"And then you'll leave me alone?"

"Of course," Kunze said.

They met about a mile north of the art museum, in a miserable little copse invisible from the main road, the site of countless low-rent love assignations and hop handoffs. The rain had been on most of the week. A bold drizzle slicked everything under an ashen sky, threatening to wash away the city in a torrent of mud and sin. Walking up the hill was like moving through sodden glue. Pritzker's umbrella provided little comfort.

Kunze waited at the top of the hill, flanked by a couple of goons. The Bund didn't function without muscle. Pritzker stood in front of him, panting.

"What's the news?" Kunze said.

"The team is playing in Scranton in about two hours," Pritzker said. "They're playing in Pittsburgh tomorrow. And they're driving the main road between the two tonight to save money."

Kunze spat on the ground. *An unnecessary move*, Pritzker thought.

"Typical," he said. "Is there anything else?"

"That's what I've got," said Pritzker.

"Good enough, then," said Kunze.

"May I ask what you intend to do with this information?"

"We have a little surprise intended for Philadelphia's favorite basketball team."

"Maybe just scare them a little?"

"We've discovered that fear isn't much of a weapon against these fellows," said Kunze. "We were thinking of harm a little more…long lasting."

At that moment, Pritzker knew that he'd done something grievously wrong. Kunze's goon—wait, weren't there two of them just a minute ago?—moved toward him, with a blackjack in hand. The rain really started to come down now.

"What are you doing?" Pritzker said, now feeling true terror for the first time in his life. "I gave you what you wanted, you bastard!"

"Not everything I wanted," said Kunze.

The threat no longer seemed abstract. They needed to fight these bastards. Pritzker was going to lead the charge. He had to warn Natalya, the SPHAs, everyone.

Pritzker took a few steps down the hill and ran into a tractor-sized Bundsman, who pushed him to the ground as if swatting a mosquito. He felt leaves in his beard and raindrops in his eyes. For a few seconds, he scrambled to his feet. Then he was down again, and sliding, grasping the side of the hill. He stopped at the feet of the first lackey, who picked Pritzker up by his collar and threw him against a rock. Pritzker felt a warm pain in his temple, and he knew he was done.

He got up on his knees one last time and shouted, "Why?" to Kunze, who was coming toward him with a grin.

"Because you're a Jew," Kunze said. "And because we could."

Pritzker felt the knife enter just under his left shoulder blade. He howled. Kunze thought they maybe should have chosen a quieter patsy. The knife dug past bone and gristle, until finally it went through Pritzker's heart. And then the corpse of David Pritzker pitched forward into a pile of leaves, to be discovered by the cops or the crows, whoever got there first. Kunze didn't worry much about the former, because he knew the guys on this beat, and the latter could have their fill.

One of Kunze's lackeys took out Pritzker's wallet, removed six dollars, and then dumped the empty wallet on the ground beside the body. They laid a fifth of scotch by Pritzker's stunned-looking face and tossed the bloody knife into the Schuylkill River. Then they walked downhill in the rain, not worried about the howls of David Pritzker's sainted mother that were sure to echo throughout suburban New Jersey when the cops finally found the rain-bloated body of what had once been her little boy.

The Jewish Students' Defense Coalition needed a new president.

• n i n e t e e n •

THE UNLIT and often unmarked 288 miles of road between Scranton and Pittsburgh sliced through some of the bleakest, most miserable, and slop-stained acreage in North America, as befit a byway connecting north-central Pennsylvania and the foothills of the Appalachians. The team car—a step van that Zinkoff had converted to hold about a dozen people—could barely go twenty-five miles per hour because of the weather and the heavy cargo, and also because it had been designed for neighborhood milk delivery, not hauling ten guys across country. Their gear weighed a ton, and the players weighed several more. A windstorm had sprung up, which didn't make driving any more pleasant.

Zinkoff moved the van through a cyclonic tunnel of howling leaves. He dodged those pretty well; they'd had the bulbs changed on the headlights before leaving Philly. But he had less luck dislodging the mud clods that kept kicking up to the windshield, splattering hard, like someone had just thrown a gopher out of a truck bed right at them. The wipers could barely budge the mud. Every fifteen minutes or so, Zink had to stop the car and wipe off the windshield using a rag that no longer really resembled cloth. The rain had soaked him through to the vest. He smelled like stale coffee brewed in a stable.

Zink had been trying for hours to get Gottlieb to call off the trip. This night wasn't fit for any activity, much less driving across what amounted to enemy territory. But Gottlieb was stubborn. He stared ahead grimly, his glowing-orange cigar tip the only sign of warmth in the dark car and the only color other than brown, black, or gray across the whole grim landscape. They had to press forward, Gottlieb said, if they wanted to be in Pittsburgh for breakfast.

They sat three to a row, with Shostack and Litwack in the front without a third guy. Litwack always got a little extra legroom, and Shostack couldn't sit in the back because of the danger that his bulk might tip the car. Inky had had better nights. He had gotten stuck in the back, lodged between Shikey and Fitch, both snoring at a rude volume. Sundodger, who could sleep not only anytime but anywhere, lay under the middle seat but kept tilting toward Inky's feet. Inky's arms were pinned to his sides. He wiggled his toes to keep the blood circulating. He would have been better off in the trunk with the dirty uniforms. In such moments, he distracted himself by thinking of Natalya. That woman made him weak. Splitting with her had been a stupid waste. He tried to wonder what she was doing now, but the cramped conditions made it tough to fantasize.

"You sure know how to show a guy a good time, Eddie," Inky said.

Gottlieb pulled his cigar out. "Don't give me that, Lautman. You get your fun sometimes. This is penance."

"I didn't know penance was in my contract."

"Gotta read the fine print," said Litwack, who had his hat drawn peacefully over his eyes.

"Fuck you, Litwack," said Inky.

Inky looked in front, behind, and to either side of him. All he could see was a sheet of dirty water, rushing down as though they were driving through a waterfall and out the other side. Gottlieb had bought a car that could stand artillery shelling, but the wet was still starting to seep in under the floorboards. The sweep of Zinkoff's headlights caught nothing but slick road ahead, occasionally illuminating a roadside scarecrow whipping around in the wind like a dervish gatekeeper to the next level of hell. Already, Inky knew that a sleepless night awaited him. He could predict the dry eyes and raw brain that would result. A few hours ago, he'd been putting the final bow on a twenty-point win, and now look at him.

Zinkoff hit a pothole that felt like a canyon. The car shucked forward, shooting Inky's upper lip into the next seat, and then hard back, thrusting the top of his head toward the ceiling. There'd be a lump. Inky thought about telling Zink to be careful, but he knew that Zink was as careful as he could be, given the lousy assignment. He'd steered the team in a hundred above and ten below. Zink righted the ship and kept on cruising.

A half hour passed, and now everyone was asleep but Inky and Zinkoff. There was no way for Inky to get comfortable unless he wanted to lie down in Fitch's lap, an act that Fitchy wouldn't respond to kindly. Mother Nature was giving him and Zink a lightning display through the windshield, the bolts dancing like some kind of after-hours extravaganza at the Grand Pavilion at the World's Fair, except that Inky didn't have a girl on his arm or a load of ice cream in his gut. Instead, it was just snoring Jews and enough rain to wash away the ark.

A big strike hit just to the left of them, followed by a thunderclap that seemed to roll across the road. They drove a couple more minutes. A series of lightning bolts exploded around them. One hit a sad little roadside sycamore. Just for a second, Inky saw them, at least a half dozen figures, backlit against the electricity, holding pitchforks and shovels, and worse.

"Hey, Zink," he said. "Did you—"

They hit another pothole, except it wasn't a pothole, because there was no dip. The car listed to starboard. There was an explosion, like a tire popping, and then another, and then Zink was whipping the wheel around, like he was having trouble controlling things. A thwack came from the lower right side. This ship wasn't going to stay upright much longer.

"Brace for impact!" Zink shouted.

The van skidded and turned. The passenger-side mirror hit a fence post. They were on the verge of capsizing. But at the last second, it righted itself and landed in the middle of the road with a great thud, leaning to one side like an old man on a cane. They sat there, idling, in the middle of the highway. They were a big dumb duck on a pond during the first day of hunting season, just waiting for someone to take a shot.

That'll wake 'em, Inky thought.

Zink cut the engine. He pulled a slicker over his head and got out, cursing. Inky told him to be careful, but Zink was in a different zone.

They'd blown two tires, maybe more. There was only one spare in the trunk. What could have done that? He walked a few feet up the flooded road, practically spitting water. Something hard crunched under his boot. Someone had scattered shards of glass and little bits of sharp metal across the road. Zink was no dummy. He'd been to college. *Shit*, he thought. *We got sabotaged.*

A crack of lightning ripped across the horizon. Zink saw figures walking down the road toward them, four in the center of the highway and at least one on either shoulder. They all carried objects that didn't look friendly. He hoofed it back to the car. All the guys were inside and awake, looking damp and acting grouchy.

"It's a setup!" he said. "Someone laid glass across the road, and they're coming!"

"Whaddya mean, they're coming?" Gottlieb said.

"I mean they're coming right now, and we gotta get out of the car or they're going to blow our brains out!"

Lightning flashed. Inky looked out the back window. Sure enough, the men he thought he'd seen earlier were approaching, and at a good pace.

"Small groups!" he said. "Encounter the enemy only if you have the element of surprise. Meet back here at dawn. Go!"

None of these guys had ever known a minute of wartime, or even service, but the SPHAs knew what it was like to be close to armed people who wanted to kill them. They were used to obeying hurried instructions in close quarters, even if those instructions involved sending them running out into the abyss in the middle of the night in a driving rain. A career playing basketball made for decent military training.

Inky was out the door fourth or fifth. He couldn't quite tell in the rush. Regardless, he was drenched, splashing as fast as he could through mud and straw across a blasted dark heath. Ahead, he saw a teammate. He drew even with him. Lightning flashed. Litwack. Could the night get any worse?

He turned around. Two of their pursuers were right behind them. One had a shovel raised over his head and was ready to bring it down on Litwack's head.

"The Bund says hello," the guy said.

"We don't accept the call," Inky replied as he spun and caught the Bundsman with a punch to the kidneys.

"Lautman!" Litwack said. "Follow me!"

Inky wanted to get the lug again, but he knew it would probably be smarter to regroup. Litwack had already moved to where the footing was a bit surer, or at least less muddy. Inky dashed to meet him. The Bundsmen chased him every step. As they ran,

Litwack pointed in the distance, a few hundred yards ahead. "There's a barn," he said. "We can make a stand."

"It's the Bund," Inky said.

"Well," said Litwack, "then we can't afford to lose."

Litwack headed over, Inky right behind him. For once, Inky was glad to be Litwack's second, especially when he heard Litwack shout in pain. Inky got closer. Litwack had run into a barbed-wire fence at a pretty good speed. The barbs had speared him in the chest and belly. He'd gotten loose there. But the fence had also grabbed him low and tight. He grunted, leaning against a post.

Behind them, the Bundsmen were closing fast. Litwack couldn't move. He'd die there, impaled in the rain. Inky had to free him fast. The outlines were getting close now in the dark.

"This is gonna hurt, Harry," he said.

"It already does!"

Inky squatted in the mud, grabbed Litwack's calves, and pulled upward. He heard a tear and hoped it was mostly cloth, but judging by the horrifying howl that Litwack had unleashed, he'd ripped some flesh. Nonetheless, Litwack was loose, if moaning a little.

"You okay?" Inky said.

"I've been better."

"We need to get over this wire—now."

Litwack placed both hands on the post, grunted, and pulled his body upward. The Bundsmen were less than a hundred yards away now. Litwack couldn't get over. His legs weren't strong enough now.

"Put one foot on the post and lift the other into my hand," Inky said. "Now!"

Fifty yards and closing.

Litwack did that.

"Pull up, hard!"

He did that as well, and then Inky thrust upward with his arms. He essentially *threw* Litwack over the fence. It wasn't easy. Litwack had thirty pounds on him. Still, he was on the other side, rolling away a little, trying to get up on his hands. The Bundsmen were very close now. Inky had no choice but to launch himself over with no support. When the top of his foot hit the wire, he felt the barbs scrape his heel. But he hadn't spent ten years doing balance drills for nothing. He leaped like a cat, and landed like one too, just as one of the Bundsmen fired. The bullet missed Inky by an inch, lodging in a post. Only the darkness was keeping them alive.

Inky scooped up Litwack and leaned him into his shoulder.

"Can you walk?" he said.

"Sort of," said Litwack.

"Looks like you'll have to follow my orders for once."

"My worst nightmare," said Litwack.

"And my fondest dream," Inky replied.

The barn sat across the field, looking inviting and dry. They could hole up there for at least a few minutes while the Bund morons figured out how to get over the fence. Lightning flashed and Inky saw them looking at the wire like two-year-olds trying to figure out a jigsaw puzzle.

Litwack could barely put any weight on his left foot; the wire had chewed up his calf pretty good. But Inky still had some strength left. He dragged Litwack alongside him. Litwack tried gamely with his one decent foot, but Inky could tell those legs were pretty raw. He barely gave any thrust at all.

Inky stepped in a big mound of mud, except that it didn't smell like mud. In the distance, he could hear cows braying. Great. Stumbling into a pile of cow flop was only the third worst thing that had happened to him in the last fifteen minutes. It was that kind of a night.

Inky and Litwack found themselves at the barn. A long wooden bolt fastened the doors, but Inky knocked that away

easily. He dragged Litwack through the entry. Every living creature within a mile that had sought shelter from the maelstrom
scurried and scratched, bailing for their secret corners. Rodents
and their predators would all remain equally hidden until the
storm passed; none of them was dumb enough to mess with the
people who'd barged in uninvited.

The barn smelled like eighteen different kinds of animal shit,
but the floor was only slightly damp. Inky could make out hay
piles and buckets and tools. *It's always good to have a fresh supply
of pitchforks*, he thought. He also spotted an oil lamp sitting on a
ledge, walked over, and was thrilled to see a dry matchbook. He
sparked it, lit the lamp, and got to see his new headquarters for
the first time. It was pretty much a barn.

Litwack collapsed onto a pile of hay, breathing hard. Inky
brought the lantern over. Litwack's knees and shins had been torn
up pretty good. But he didn't see bone, and there wasn't a ton of
blood. Inky tore strips off the bottoms of Litwack's pants, which
were pretty ruined anyway, and turned them into wet makeshift
bandages. Litwack grunted a little—Inky was sure it hurt—but he
didn't make a ton of noise. *This guy's pretty tough*, Inky thought.
He banished that sentiment quickly. Admiring Litwack didn't
really fit into his rock-hard worldview. Still, in that night of need,
that hour of desperation, the bonds of blood made these men,
these sons of hard times, feel something like brotherhood but
deeper and more ancient, an eternal seal that couldn't be broken, not even by rivalry. They were Jews, and that counted for
something.

"You know, Lautman," Litwack said, "you might put on a
tough facade, but you're a pretty decent guy."

"Eat my ass, pretty boy," Inky said.

"Not even for dessert," said Litwack.

Inky wondered how the other guys were faring, and he especially worried that Gottlieb wasn't really equipped to escape a

situation like this. Was he tough? Sure. Or at least he had been, in his prime. But if Inky already felt like a three-hundred-pound bag of wet cement, then how could Gottlieb possibly be doing? He didn't have the legs to run in weather like this.

The door to the barn burst open to reveal an answer. Inky rolled to his right and popped up, fists cocked. It was Shostack, breathing like a buffalo, carrying Eddie Gottlieb on his back as though he were a schoolboy and the coach a mildly heavy book bag. Gottlieb's head lolled from side to side, and he moaned softly. Shostack lowered Gottlieb onto a pile of hay in a far corner of the barn.

"Is he all right?" Inky said.

"He's alive," Shostack said. "But let's just say the night air didn't agree with him."

Zinkoff followed behind, panting and looking haunted, like a runaway bride fleeing a hillbilly wedding.

He bolted the door.

"Five huge, angry farm boys are bearing down on us," he said. "At least three guns. I think one of them's got an ax."

"It's the Bund," Inky said. "Someone set us up."

"Ach," Gottlieb groaned. "The Bund!"

Shostack noticed Litwack.

"What happened to him?" he said.

"He met a fence he didn't like."

"Why didn't you go through the gate like we did?" Shostack asked.

"We were in a hurry," Litwack said. "We didn't really have time to take a land survey."

"You could probably use this, then," Shostack said, pulling Gottlieb's flask out of his coat pocket.

Litwack took a grateful slug and then another. He passed the flask to Inky, who had himself a long pull as well. *We're three able-bodied men*, he thought, *against what looks like five.* He looked at

Zinkoff, who was dabbing his forehead with a wet kerchief and moaning like a cat in heat. *All right*, Inky rethought, *not exactly three.*

They heard a shotgun loading outside. Zinkoff yelped. Inky'd have to plan quickly, or they wouldn't see another dawn.

twenty

THE DOOR exploded open and the Bundsmen stepped into darkness. They'd seen the mountain-sized guy carrying the fat guy into here, and knew they didn't have a way out. But there was no evidence of their targets. The sound was only crickets, mixed with a steady downpour.

A bucket flew out of the dark and hit one of them in the face. He yowled in pain and dropped his shotgun. The rest of them moved in. They heard a noise overhead and turned around. Inky dropped from the rafters like a cat, knocking them off balance. When they spun around, they ran into a wall of Shostack, who knocked two of them together like bowling pins. Zinkoff swung his bucket in the dark, landing blows where he could.

One Bundsman, faster than the others, was holding an ax; he ran through the open space, running his blade through the hay, hoping to get lucky. His foot met another foot and he tripped, landing on his stomach. A lightning strike illuminated the scene for a second. Eddie Gottlieb emerged from the hay, a fat devil holding a pitchfork. He plunged it at the guy's ass.

"You fucked with my tour!" Gottlieb said.

He made contact. The thug screamed. That'd hold him down.

A gun went off. Shostack had fired it, and one of the Bund guys had gone down.

Meanwhile, Inky and a Bundsman were going at it pretty good on the other side of the barn, landing blows where they could. Inky took one pretty hard on the jaw. This guy had probably boxed some, he realized.

"Charlie!" he said. "A little help here?"

Shostack came over and smacked the guy on the forehead. The guy went down like Raggedy Andy. There were only two left standing now. The one with the gun had stopped firing because he was out of bullets, and the other was cowering in the corner while Zinkoff beat him with a bucket. Zink, in his excitement, made a noise so shrill and obnoxious that a tomcat shot out of the hay, howling, and ran out into the soggy night rather than listen to any more.

That left only one, who stood in the middle of the barn, shivering and holding a pistol. Inky lit the lamp. Shostack came up behind the guy and held him in a bear grip.

"Oh look," Inky said, "a poor little lamb that's lost his way. Baa baa baa."

The guy spit in Inky's face. Inky slapped him.

"Who sent you?" Inky said.

"Your mother," said the guy.

Shostack squeezed harder. Inky punched the guy in the gut.

"I don't think she has your number. Now tell me who gave the order to attack us, or Charlie here will use you for accordion practice."

On cue, Shostack constricted his grip, about to crush his prey. The guy wheezed and cursed and looked about ready to pass out. Shostack let him go.

"Kunze," he said.

"That snake," said Gottlieb.

"Were you supposed to kill us or scare us?"

"Both," said the guy. "He told us to pile you all in a ditch without a note."

"Nice," Inky said. "Harry, you want to take care of this guy?"

"Sure," came a voice from the darkness.

Litwack stood up from the hay. He limped forward, leaned on Inky's shoulder for support, pumped his fist, leveled an uppercut, and sent the guy sprawling. Anyone else who came through that barn door would get the same.

Shostack and Inky stood guard in the barn all night so Litwack and Gottlieb and Zink could get a little rest. They'd found a roll of baling twine and had tied the Bund guys tight. The rain stopped around dawn, about the time they heard roosters and crows. They gathered the crew and left the Bund guys in the barn, bolting the door. They'd stay there a few hours, until a very surprised farmer opened it up to fetch a bag of seed.

The Jews had straw in their hair and fuzz in their brains. The field had already begun to steam. Hawks circled overhead, evidence that a day of sunny hunting was on the horizon. The air smelled new. Crops would grow well out here this season.

It seemed like they'd run forever the night before, but the road was really only a few hundred feet away, which was good, because dragging Litwack along was making Inky tired. The car sat where they'd left it, in the middle of the road, both front tires shredded. Fitch, Gothofer, and Rosan, who'd gone in another direction, leaned on the front bumper, looking proud. Shikey stood with his foot on top of yet another Bundsman. They'd bound his hands and feet with spare netting from the equipment bag and had stuffed a wet kerchief in his mouth.

"Good morning!" Fitch said. "Did you sleep well?"

"We made a night of it," Gottlieb said.

"You look real nice, Eddie."

"I'm gonna dock your pay, you ingrate."

"I see you caught a field mouse," said Inky.

"He didn't run far," said Shikey. "A weak little thing."

"We've got his burrow mates in the barn," said Gottlieb. "Charlie, you mind hauling him back?"

"Not at all, boss."

Shostack, ever loyal and ever strong, loaded the guy up on his back and took him to join the rest. The guy barely protested. Lord knows what they'd done to him in the night.

"Where's Sundodger?" Inky asked.

Fitch jerked a thumb toward the car. Sundodger was snoring away, splayed across the backseat. That guy could sleep through anything. Inky opened the door and tickled the backs of his knees.

"Wakey, wakey, Sundodger," he said.

Sundodger didn't move.

"I got a piece of cooze here who wants to get to know you."

Sundodger opened one eye just to make sure. When he determined that, as usual, there weren't any dames around, just a bunch of smelly jocks, he closed it again.

"Did I miss anything?" he said.

"Nope, you were on the bench during all the action," said Inky. "As usual."

"That's good."

A farm truck came by within the hour. The SPHAs all got freshly picked apples. Inky and Litwack rode to the next town so they could order a tow and get Harry patched. The repair truck came and they got the tires fixed. They were in Pittsburgh for lunch, a shower, and the greatest nap any of them had ever taken, even if it was on cots in the gym of the Pittsburgh JCC, which was putting them up for free.

If they won that night, Gottlieb said, he'd take them all out for steaks. It'd be tough, he thought, because Litwack wouldn't play and would probably be out for a week.

But the SPHAs won by a dozen. It would have been more, but they missed their last four shots on purpose just to give Gottlieb false hope that the other team might stage a comeback. Gottlieb had to learn to stop making bets he couldn't win. He paid for dinner, reluctantly.

twenty-one

CHICAGO SMELLED like pigs, whiskey, and money. Inky liked it there. East Coast cities had energy, but the people were rats scrambling for a piece of cheese thrown into a cage. The middle of the country acted either too respectable or too scared. And the South, though Inky liked the food and the women, seemed burdened by some sort of heavy sadness that he couldn't name. He'd never been much farther west than he was right now, so he couldn't speak to its regional character. Chicago, though, just moved through the day not caring much about the rest of the world, a mentality Inky could well understand. When Chicago woke up, it was the only city, and it always went to bed satisfied.

Inky guessed Gottlieb was feeling pretty flush at the moment, because he checked them into a hotel on Wabash that had fresh-cut flowers in night-table vases. Gottlieb put them two to a room. Inky didn't complain, because he'd been sleeping for a week in the car with his schnozz in Shostack's armpit. Inky did have some nagging concerns. Eddie obviously wasn't going to pay back his debt, but it also wasn't going to look good if he started running around like Wallis Simpson on holiday.

On his way out to get something to eat and smoke, Inky saw Eddie in the hotel lobby.

"Pretty fancy digs here, Eddie," he said. "What gives?"

"I thought you fellows deserved something special," said Gottlieb.

"I won't argue," said Inky. "Except I will. This ain't your money."

"No court in the country's gonna convict me for welshing on a Bund loan," Eddie said. "Don't worry. There are plans."

"Your last plan nearly got me killed in a cornfield."

"These are improved plans."

"They'd better be."

"Zinkoff and I are driving up to Wisconsin for a couple of days. For scouting. And to air out the car."

"Oh, come on, Eddie. You just want to eat sausages and cheese curds."

"That's a side benefit."

Inky looked unconvinced. Eddie pulled him close.

"I know this place in Lake Geneva that has a Finnish masseuse. She's got hands like anvils. And there are two separate hot pools," he said. "I'll take you there sometime."

"But meanwhile," Inky said, "I've got to stay in Chicago and play basketball."

"It could be worse," Gottlieb said.

"That is true," said Inky.

"You'll have fun. I'll take care of you."

"Okay, Eddie."

"By the way, Litwack's coaching while I'm gone."

It was worse.

Gottlieb hadn't told them much about what or whom they'd be facing in Chicago, only that it would be a surprise. Eddie had activated the carnival barker side of his personality. His surprises rarely meant dignity for those involved. Once, he'd gotten a local pickle manufacturer to sponsor a game and donate special uniforms with the firm's name on the back. Inky had smelled like garlic, brine, and vinegar for a week. As opening acts to basketball, Inky had seen midget wrestlers, an a cappella group of Italian castrati, and a guy who could play a trumpet with his toes. One afternoon, he'd found himself at the grand opening of a Baltimore furniture store, matching wits with a tic-tac-toe-playing chicken. Life's humiliations never ended.

Litwack had the team take cabs up Lake Shore Drive to its northern terminus. They parked in the roundabout driveway of a twenty-story building painted bright pink, with a ten-story tower sticking out the center like a middle finger extended toward the poorer districts inland. The air was cloudless, in the high sixties, and the city had emerged like Persephone from her seasonal prison. Across the road, Lake Michigan extended wavelessly toward an unknown horizon. Polish women with legs like uncooked spring lambs sat on the beach in their housedresses, gossiping and occasionally rooting around in the trash cans for treasure. Their children were sticky with freshwater and sand. The SPHAs blinked into the sun and marveled that a beach this nice should be so uncrowded. On the East Coast, people swarmed to the shore like bugs on a sugar-water spill. Here, they just had light winds from the north and a few prosperous immigrant couples pushing their prams along the sidewalk.

A Woody Herman record played in the lobby. Colored porters took the team's equipment out of the trunk and led them inside, to the ballroom where they'd be playing. The court had already been set up—no chicken wire, an actual electric scoreboard, and the first few rows of seats had padding. Art hung on the freshly painted walls, and there were polished chandeliers overhead. One floor down, each player got his own locker, and the room came with three soaking tubs. Gottlieb had arranged for a massage table and fruit baskets and bottled beer on ice.

Athletes should *be treated so well*, Inky thought. *We work hard.* He felt pampered and alive. There had to be a catch. And there was.

They went upstairs for afternoon drills. While Gottlieb got his flab rubbed in his Wisconsin hideaway, the SPHAs passed medicine balls back and forth until their shoulders ached. They practiced set shots, yawning with boredom. Litwack had planned the program. He drilled with the team as much as he could. Even with his bum gams, he still liked a workout. This was one of his essential leadership qualities that Inky couldn't stand.

Inky wasn't about to let Litwack give him any notes. In the scrimmage, Inky ran the point like a chemist pouring acid. Not a drop went where it wasn't supposed to go, and the formula came out right. Litwack knew this about Inky and gave him a wide berth. Inky knew that Litwack knew.

The action stopped as soon as the other team came out of its locker room, wearing red-and-white uniforms so shiny they reflected the late-afternoon sun. They ran to the opposite side of the court, not acknowledging the SPHAs at all, and began their drills, just like any other team.

Inky gaped. He would have been more surprised if he'd seen reindeer playing basketball. Every last one of them was a creature he'd never before seen on a basketball court.

Dames.

In the Ozarks, there lived a druggist named Olson who loved basketball. Olson taught himself the behind-the-back pass, and he got pretty good at it too. He had a knack for the game and a mind for business. His Cassville, Missouri, drugstore became the headquarters for a barnstorming team called the Terrible Swedes, which lived up to its name. The Swedes did okay regionally, but every time they'd venture north and east, they'd come home with a regrettable collection of twenty-point losses, not to mention a surplus of welts and bruises, like a retreating Confederate battalion after an ill-planned raid on a Union weapons depot.

Olson found himself surrounded by incompetent men. The women of his region, on the other hand, had fists like hammers, legs like railroad ties, and a genetic predisposition toward taking punches. The Ozarks bred independent ladies who could lift heavy. In that verdant, elevated hillbilly cradle, the sport of women's basketball germinated and flowered. Women's AAU teams left the local men sucking wind by the second quarter, to the point where the men stopped scheduling exhibitions. Olson's eye for talent attached itself to them.

He recruited the best for a traveling gig. Four of the first five ladies had red hair, so he called his team the All American Red Heads. The rest got their hair dyed with henna; Olson's wife owned a chain of beauty parlors in Missouri and Arkansas. The players worked in the beauty racket in the off-season if they needed the job, which most of them did.

Meanwhile, they traveled 180 days a year, getting paid to play basketball. The conventional wisdom of the age went that the female game should operate differently from the male one, because if women played like men did, it'd hurt their chances to have children. This flat-out lie led to a weird hybrid game in which the women played six-on-six, with the court divided into three sections. Only three players for each team got to play at a time in the active area near either one of the hoops, while the rest waited their turns in the middle, like seconds in a relay race. Offside calls and foot faults abounded, which added a plodding tightrope-walk element to the game. The Red Heads went about dismantling the rule and the myths that led to its creation.

Their traveling schedule meant they took on men's teams, with men's rules, most of the time. They only won about half their games. Sometimes the men were just bigger and stronger. More often, the men would cheat because the idea of being beaten by a team of henna-dyed ladies was just too humiliating for their fragile egos. Either way, Olson had found a cash cow, and he milked its teats, hard. They traveled everywhere, including a yearly trip to Hollywood, where they got Cesar Romero's autograph and one of the more attractive numbers went to the Brown Derby with Tyrone Power. In smaller towns, the Red Heads could draw upwards of a thousand paying customers for their games, crowds beaten only by the county fair or a Bob Wills show if he came to town, which he never did.

Eddie Gottlieb, always with an eye on the main chance, got wind of Olson's lady basketball shenanigans and called him up at the drugstore.

"Olson!" said Gottlieb.

"Yes?" said Olson.

"Eddie Gottlieb here, from Philadelphia."

"I've heard of you, Mr. Gottlieb."

"Let's talk basketball."

"My favorite topic, sir."

"So my boys are cruising through Chicago soon on tour. And we're tired of our usual exhibitions against the University of Chicago varsity team. They're slow and uninspired."

"I can see how that would be the case. So how can I help?"

"Well, I hear that you have some lady players who give the men a hard time on the court."

"We like to think so," Olson said.

"How about a deal?"

"Maybe."

"Three games in three nights, with a sixty-forty door split in my favor, because I'll do all the work. You just have to get your ladies there."

"All right, then."

Gottlieb gave the date.

"Ah, but there's a problem," Olson said. "We have a game scheduled in Texarkana that weekend. I can, however, send up my junior team, the Ozark Hillbillies, which has some fine up-and-coming talent."

"The SPHAs are champions," Gottlieb said. "We don't play second-rate teams."

"Well, it sounds like you'll be playing a second-rate team from the University of Chicago that weekend."

Olson heard a loud sigh, followed by what sounded suspiciously like a head hitting a desk. After a few seconds, Gottlieb's voice returned.

"All right," Eddie said. "A fifty-fifty split, with five hundred bucks guaranteed."

"For that kind of money," Olson said, "I think we can change our schedule."

The Red Heads ran through their layup drills with a little extra mustard on the ball. They shot well and dribbled clean. But even though they looked good warming up, the SPHAs couldn't help laughing. Shikey and Rosan and Fitch were doubled up in the corner. Kaselman ran his hand through his hair, hoping to draw attention to his devil-may-care ways. Shostack shyly retreated into the shadows. And Inky just stared in disbelief.

"Broads?" he said. "Eddie's got us playing *broads*?"

Litwack, who was still running the show while Gottlieb got his nails manicured, came up alongside.

"They're going to make *you* look like a broad if you don't take them seriously," Litwack said.

"Get lost, Litwack."

That night, the Red Heads showed their stuff. Because of the strange rules of women's basketball, they'd adapted passing patterns that the SPHAs didn't know how to defend. They played only five women on the court at a time. But it seemed like six. Though they didn't shoot much from the outside because of the long arms of the SPHAs, they didn't need that kind of offensive help; they moved around the court in planned loops, swarming like bees, handing the ball off and making strange little hop passes to the open gal in the lane, who always seemed ready to convert for an easy one-handed layup. Shostack was too slow in the center to stop them.

On the offensive side, Inky made a couple of shots and the short game worked okay, but they couldn't get the ball inside much. Litwack sat on the bench, orchestrating the action poorly. If he'd been in there, they would have had an extra threat. He was the only one with a decent inside-outside game, which is what the SPHAs desperately needed.

The Red Heads were sneaky little pickpockets. They had the SPHAs sweating and on their heels. Nothing Litwack called out seemed to work. The crowd roared every time the Red Heads did something embarrassing to the men. Inky could almost hear Gottlieb laughing from his Wisconsin hide-away, both because he liked to show his team up from time to time and because he was obviously bringing in a ton of money tonight. The halftime buzzer went off, and the SPHAs were down 20–11.

"Damn," Shostack said as they went into the locker room. "Those broads are kicking our ass."

A broad skittered past.

"Maybe next time you won't give us such an inviting target," she said, swatting his behind.

"I think she likes you, Charlie," Inky said.

"Shut up, Inky," said Shostack.

In the lockers, the SPHAs figured out some things. The dames liked to do their little switch-and-roll trick somewhere between the top of the key and half-court, which eventually drew the whole defense up so that one or two of them could slip behind the lines for a layup. Leave someone, preferably someone big, to patrol under the hoop, Litwack said, and that problem would be solved. On offense, check twice, like a kid crossing the street, before making a pass. Work the ball tight and inside, and make them claw at you high. The Red Heads had one player about Inky's height, and Inky was the shortest guy on the team. No one else came within three inches. The SPHAs were taller, stronger, and faster. Now they had to play smarter. Then they could go out there and defeat those women.

The strategy worked for a while. Inky swiped the ball at midcourt and drove for a score. He threaded the needle with his passing, even though the Red Heads played lower to the ground than any opponent he could remember, and he couldn't always get the passes through. He cut the lead to five, then three, then one. But they hadn't counted on the fact that the Red Heads could shoot and didn't wholly need to rely on tricks. And the SPHAs couldn't throw elbows. These were *women*, after all.

The Red Heads often counted on this weakness of men as a conduit to victory. They could have taken elbows to the chops as well as anyone, but they didn't put that on their calling cards. The SPHAs scored a lot in the second half, but the Red Heads scored enough themselves. When Misty Carruthers drained a fifteen-foot set shot with ten seconds left, the lid closed. The Red Heads won 40–35. The crowd applauded as the Red Heads took a bow. Rather than sulk back to the basement, the SPHAs applauded too. Why not? They hadn't had this much fun playing basketball in a long time.

The teams shook hands for the press. Kaselman put his long arms around some buff Red Head shoulders and grinned for the cameras. Inky got down and made hotshot hand gestures with the Red Heads' point guard.

"Good game," she said. "But not good enough."

"We held back," he said.

"They always say that."

"It doesn't matter," he said. "Because we got paid."

"They always say that too," she said. "Meet us at the hotel later. We'll play for the real stakes."

It turned out that the Red Heads were pretty good at poker, and they could smoke cigars too. Quite a party got going there on Wabash after all the employees, save one tired-looking bohunk bartender, had gone home. Olson gave his girls a line of credit at the bar, which he often did when they won, and they spent it lavishly on Canadian whiskey and Missourian beer.

There were twelve of them and seven SPHAs. Litwack went to bed soon after they got home, taking just enough time to offer a toast and to down a shot to help him sleep. Kaselman sat on a couch, one arm each around the Red Heads' most gamine-looking numbers. They giggled in his grasp. Shostack sat across from him with the Red Heads' center. She had a sweet disposition and the face and body of an ice-truck mare. They were snuggling noisily like bears in heat, a sight that everyone else in the room tried to ignore. The rest of the SPHAs divided up at poker, enough to make two tables of seven. They figured, wrongly again, to take these dames for an easy score.

Inky sat at one of the tables, listlessly sipping on his watery drink, entering the fray only if he had high pocket pairs or suited face cards. Having all these gals around was making him sick. He knew how it worked on the road. Everyone was going to pair off tonight, and he didn't want any part. His heart was a windowless room without furniture. It felt stripped bare, cold and lonely. He'd been rude and selfish and cruel to Natalya, and she'd been annoying, pompous, and defensive, yet his every thought was about her, as though she'd authored them herself. Inky didn't need Natalya to tell him to love her, because it was there, as plain as the sky or the morning paper. He hadn't seen her for a while, but she was still more present than anything else. Every night was death, and every day purgatory. Inky had spent his whole life taking his feelings and putting them away, hoarding them like spare pennies. Now they wouldn't stop spilling out, lost memories rattling his soul in a continual loop. Time moved forward or backward or whatever time does, but in Inky's mind, he and Natalya were forever.

The bet came around to him. He didn't notice. Rosan had to give him a nudge under the table. Inky looked at his pocket jacks. A good enough play, but who cared? He'd made the worst bet of his life the day he'd let Natalya walk away.

"Fold," he said.

He must have given the sigh of his life then, because the action stopped. Even the bartender stopped clinking his ice. There Inky Lautman sat, wretched and guilty, at the bottom of his own personal well.

The Red Head to his left touched his arm gently.

"Honey," she said, "just call her."

She was right. Inky got up and went to a phone booth in the lobby. He gave the operator the Shostack number in the Philly exchange. Natalya answered on the first ring. She'd been waiting every night by the phone until at least two, sometimes later. They had a lot to talk about.

twenty-two

INKY'S REUNION conversation with Natalya wasn't exactly kisses and light. This made it easier, somehow. They had more important business than their feelings. She'd been trying to get in touch with him for days.

Pritzker was dead. The cops had found his body in the park and had no leads. But Natalya thought she knew, because she'd been the last one to see Pritzker alive. He'd been asking weird questions about the SPHAs' travel schedule. Inky knew full well that the Bund didn't mind buying off vulnerable Jews. His killing, all the way down to the fact that whoever did Pritzker in had attacked him from behind, smelled like the handiwork of one man to him.

"Kunze," he said.

"Who?" she said.

"A guy I know," he said, "who I hope you never meet."

"Inky, do you think they're watching me too?" she asked.

"They might be. Keep in mind that they're not smart enough to watch anyone for very long."

"Still," she said.

"Still," he said. "Why'd you give us up to Pritzker?"

"Because I was mad at you, Inky. And he was the head of the Jewish Students' Defense Coalition. How was I supposed to know he was working for the Bund?"

"You weren't."

Inky was the forgiving type. When it came to Natalya.

"I'm scared, Inky."

"I bet."

"I don't want to be here."

"You don't have to be."

"What do you mean?"

"I'll wire you money in the morning. Get on the noon train. We'll shack up. Shostack can have his own room."

"Are you sure you want me there?"

"Very sure."

"I've always wanted to see Chicago."

"It's pretty nice here. At least the part we're in."

Inky spent the next day doing errands to prepare. There were plans. He had to borrow a little from Shostack because Gottlieb wasn't going to pay them until he got back from his rarified Wisconsin spa.

That night, the SPHAs gave the Red Heads a fierce basketball beating. They weren't going to get taken by a ladies' team twice. Then they went back to the hotel and lost to those same ladies at poker. Inky took the elevator to his room and listened to the clock ticking. His gut was light and weak, the top of a fresh cream puff. He sensed the outlines of some undefined fate just beyond his comprehension. This was love. Inky didn't like it much. A hard shot to the jaw would have felt better.

At five a.m., he bathed, shaved, pressed a crease into his pants, went downstairs, where the poker game was still going strong, and took a cab to Union Station. The board showed Natalya's train was forty-five minutes late. Inky bought a spring mix from the flower stand.

Finally, they announced the train. She came down the platform with her little bag, looking so young and smart and pale and hopeful and just crazy enough to travel nineteen hours on a train to see a guy whom she'd sworn off forever less than two weeks before. They saw each other and ran, and then embraced so hard, and for so long, that a cop had to actually blow his whistle. This was the Midwest, after all, and such things were best done in private.

They got to the hotel. Natalya clawed at Inky in the elevator. He held her firm. They burst through his room door and onto the bed, panting. Shostack came out of the bathroom, brushing his teeth.

"Natalya!" he said. "What are you doing here?"

Shostack had been bumbling into her room unannounced for most of Natalya's life. She puffed softly, as though she were ten and writing in her diary and he was a thirteen-year-old lummox staggered by hormones.

"I'm with Inky," she said. "What about you, Charlie?"

"Why are you with Inky?" he said, between brushes.

"Because we're in love."

"That's news."

"Dammit, Shostack," Inky said. "I told you to bunk with Sundodger."

"He's got those basketball dames in his room," said Shostack. "Two. Maybe even three. You weren't here, so I took the liberty."

"Well, could you leave now?"

Shostack looked at Inky and Natalya on the bed. They regarded him coldly. He seemed to finally realize what was happening.

"Let me finish drying my hair," he said.

Soon after, word got out quickly among the hotel staff. Avoid the left wing of the fifth floor. All kinds of strange gruntings and slappings and screamings were coming from inside the walls of room 504. It stopped for ten or fifteen minutes at a time and then renewed at even greater volume. A lamp shattered. It sounded like feeding time in the lion cage.

In the dim late-afternoon light, Inky and Natalya sat up in bed, smoking. The room looked like Inky's rooms often looked, only this time there hadn't been a fight. He and Natalya crossed, and recrossed, the thin line between passion and violence and had decided on passion. It had exploded like a torpedo in there. Inky's thighs hurt. Natalya's thighs hurt. They had no words. Only quiet satisfaction.

There was a pounding at the door.

"Lautman!" a voice went. "Get your ass down to the car! We got a game in three hours!"

Gottlieb had returned. Inky stood and went to the door. He opened it, not all the way.

"Not playing tonight, Eddie," he said. "I got company."

"I don't care if you've got Myrna Loy hog-tied and begging for more. Litwack's out again, and you're playing!"

"Shit," Inky said.

He looked back into the room. Natalya waved her hand, granting permission.

"I need to clean up, Eddie. I'll take a cab and meet you there in forty-five minutes."

"The hell you will!"

"All right. I'll be downstairs in five. But I need twenty bucks to pay for this lamp I broke."

Eddie pulled a fat wad of bills out of his breast pocket. Chicago had been good to all of them. Inky wondered if maybe they were getting soft too quickly.

"You're going to kill me, Lautman," he said.

"Probably not today," Inky said.

"Probably not," said Eddie.

"Also, I got a guest."

"I figured as much."

"It's Shostack's sister."

"That, I did not figure."

Back in the room, Inky and Natalya scrambled into their clothes, smelling like each other's sweat.

"I love you, Inky," she said.

"I love you too, babe," he said.

"Well," she said.

Then came the words that Inky had been both planning and avoiding for months.

"You wanna get married?" he asked.

"Only to you."

"How about tomorrow? I got a judge lined up."

"That's pretty soon. I'd like to tell my mother."

"You can call her in the morning."

"She'll probably want to come."

"We can get married again when we get home. I don't want you to change your mind."

Natalya put her arms around his neck.

"Why would I do that?"

"Because I'm a professional basketball player who beats up guys on the side."

She kissed him.

"You're more than that to me."

"If you say so."

"I do," she said.

The SPHAs had a good game that night, beating the Redheads by ten. They rarely lost two in a row. Inky Lautman and Natalya Shostack were married the next afternoon at Chicago's city hall. Her brother, Gottlieb, Zinkoff, the rest of the SPHAs, and a half dozen All American Red Heads served as witnesses. Inky wore his other suit, Natalya a cute floral-print cornflower-blue dress that she'd bought that morning at Marshall Field's. Inky gave her a simple gold band as a placeholder to something fancier. Gottlieb caught the bouquet and threw it back. Afterward, they all went up to a deli on Roosevelt and gorged on heaping platters of brisket and rye bread and pickles. They drank a lot of wine, and then they went to see Louis Armstrong play at a club on Michigan.

But the vacation would end soon. The Bund still loomed up north, just a week away. The SPHAs were like soldiers on leave, getting ready to head back to the front.

Inky said to his wife, "How'd you like to honeymoon in Minnesota?"

PART THREE

MINNEAPOLIS

• t w e n t y - t h r e e •

KUNZE GOT off the bus with one hundred dollars and an address written on the back of an old laundry slip. The money would easily get him through a week if he spent like a Jew. The address could get him a lot more.

Minneapolis was all smoke and bricks and drugstores. Kunze had never felt air this cold before. It got real frigid in the East sometimes, but there was always a dampness that heralded something else, even if that something was a tuberculosis outbreak. But this felt as though all the oxygen had been sucked away and replaced with some sort of substance whose only purpose was to freeze human lymph. And it was April. He couldn't imagine what this place was like in December.

The ride up from Chicago had been long and cold and cramped. A man as wide as a farmhouse had gotten on at LaCrosse. He'd sat down next to Kunze, pressing against him with his massive hips and his smelly overalls. Rye reeked from his every pore. He started snoring immediately, drowning Kunze in the waft of his sour breath. Now, eight hours and no sleep later, Kunze felt disoriented, like he'd just walked onto the dock at Lisbon after a stowaway month in the lower decks of a tramp steamer. But this was the moment. It had arrived. He needed to get his brain straight.

He went into a diner across the street and ordered coffee and a fried-egg sandwich. He sipped the coffee, which had sludge in the bottom, until he felt a little life creep into his veins. When the sandwich came, he ate it in four bites. Then he ordered another sandwich and another cup of coffee.

He showed the waitress the address on the laundry slip. She said it was four or five miles away, in a nice part of town. He asked her to call him a cab; she gave him a number and told him to call it himself. She was a surly bitch, but then again, she worked in a diner across from the bus station, so he couldn't expect much more. It's not like he was Cary Grant waltzing up to the captain's table.

The cab ride cost a buck, and he tipped the cabbie an extra buck. This was the kind of neighborhood where dentists and lawyers lived. The air was just as cold here but smelled like fresh money. They pulled up in front of a wide-porch Craftsman, red-brick with a sloped roof, shingles painted dark green. It had a gray-yellow lawn, dead from a six-month harsh-weather beating, that still bore a light dusting of snow like a patch of frosted cereal. Kunze got out. Pelley lived here.

William Dudley Pelley made the rest of America's home-grown fascists look like potato farmers. After an uneventful early life, at the age of twenty-eight he went to Russia as a magazine correspondent. But while someone like John Reed could make the same trip and witness a people's revolution, Pelley drew other conclusions. He saw Ukrainian children butchered by death squads. The streets ran with blood and the gutters were stuffed with limbs. Pelley blamed the Jews. He was convinced that the atrocities he'd witnessed were just the first stage in a Talmudic conspiracy to overrun the world. Where those opinions had first set seed, it's hard to say. Perhaps he'd read a misguided pamphlet as a boy. Regardless, he filed a few articles and returned home.

Pelley started turning out novels in the 1920s. Two of his short stories won O. Henry Awards, and he tasted success. When writers get that first snack, they start hungering for the banquet. So he moved to Hollywood and wrote a couple of successful Lon Chaney pictures. Then the Hollywood work started to dry up, like it does, toward the end of the decade. The studios were full of Stalinist sympathizers, but Pelley knew the truth about Russia. He'd witnessed, firsthand, the machinations of the Bolshevik death squads. Again, Pelley blamed the Jews. He rented a bungalow in Altadena, at the foot of Mount Lowe, to work on a book about racial history.

What happened next, Pelley described in a 1929 magazine article titled "Seven Minutes in Eternity." In the middle of the night, he'd cried out, "I'm dying! I'm dying!" But no one was around to hear him. He felt himself overwhelmed by emotion and the sensation of going out of his body. He awoke, he wrote, in a realm filled with a blue light that glowed out from the core of the world. Then he proceeded to meet several deceased acquaintances and other people with whom he had profound conversations. As he later wrote in a book titled *Why I Believe the Dead Are Alive*, Pelley felt that the "mystic curtain suddenly rolled backward and showed me something of the colossal, beautiful machinery that operates—as I call it—behind physical life."

He moved to New York City, as often happens after a profound metaphysical experience, and set up shop as a medium. People paid a few bucks to go to his rented apartment for "paranormal automatic writing experiences." Pelley hired a lady medium to give the proceedings some authenticity. He later published a book about this phase that he called *Star Guests*. Meanwhile, he still blamed the Jews for everything.

Pelley had built up a pretty solid propaganda network for himself over the years, and he began using his pulpit to scare people. The Depression was on, and Jews were easy targets. In 1932, Pelley established the Silver Shirt Legion. They wore, as their name implied, silver shirts with an *L* over the right breast pocket, and they marched around and said loud, anti-Semitic things. The movement grew fast. His followers could number in the high five digits. Pelley was a real hotshot. In certain cities, he could get a serious rally together.

Minneapolis had it rough in the thirties, like most places. There was no work, but the Jews seemed to be doing all right. They'd shown up in big numbers in the early 1900s. The area around Third and Washington started smelling like schmaltz and kishke. Honestly, the food wasn't all that different from the German and Nordic food that dominated some of the older ethnic neighborhoods; it's not like these Jews had migrated from Baghdad or something. But it was different enough to annoy the previous generation of immigrants, and Pelley had more than a thousand registered Silver Shirts in the Twin Cities alone. Pelley didn't live here full-time, but he kept a house for various activities, some fascist and some metaphysical.

Pelley was the right guy for Kunze. Together, Kunze thought, they could maybe drive the SPHAs down. There was a rally scheduled for tomorrow night, right before the basketball game. The humiliation would be complete and final. This was Kunze's hope as he rang the doorbell.

A fat housekeeper answered and put a finger to her lips. Kunze found this a strange gesture, but he complied. The house was all dark woods and imported rugs. A floor-to-ceiling mirror connected to a built-in entryway coat tree had hooks hanging from it like an elk's horns.

Kunze was escorted into a parlor off the entryway. About ten women, all of them middle-aged and all of them well-heeled, were gathered in a circle around a wooden table. At the table, Pelley sat writing furiously on a paper tablet, tearing off one piece and tossing it toward his audience as he started writing on another. He was about fifty years old, five feet seven inches, and would have weighed 130 pounds in a dust storm. His black hair was smoked with gray. He kept a silver mustache and a salt-and-pepper Vandyke. A wanted poster from his regular hometown of Asheville, North Carolina, had described Pelley's dark-gray eyes as "very penetrating." A pair of wire-rimmed glasses fit tightly over a straight Roman nose. His suit was impeccably tailored, his hair perfectly combed.

"These are the messages I have received," he said, "from a source past my control and past my earthly powers, a source that resides in a place where the blue light, a light that none of us can touch, glows eternally. And I give them as my gift to you."

Kunze's mouth opened into a wide O. This was his first encounter with Pelley's metaphysical side. He found himself wondering if he'd maybe tossed in his chips on the wrong hand. His doubt grew as Pelley whipped off his glasses and beheld his rapt audience with a fiery gaze.

"BEHOLD!" Pelley said. "The greatness of eternity, the thing that exists beyond space and time and reason and history. It lives both inside and outside yourself, simultaneously of you and not of you. Fear it, love it, embrace it as your own, and know that it will persist long after you, and I, and everyone we've ever known, has been erased from the earth."

Gott im Himmel, Kunze thought.

"This, then," Pelley said, "is my blessing to you."

Pelley slumped in a chair, as though his soul suddenly had left him. A couple of hairs hung down his forehead. The ladies stood up silently, placing tens and twenties in a basket as they reverently studied their Pelley-channeled writings. To them, he was the true source of wisdom. To Kunze, he was the bankroll.

A minute or so passed. The ladies left. Pelley inhaled sharply, like a drowning man resuscitated. He looked around the room a couple of times, dabbed his forehead with a monogrammed handkerchief, slipped his glasses back over his nose, and looked up, totally composed.

"Now then, Mr. Kunze," he said, "what are we going to do about the Jews?"

• t w e n t y - f o u r •

THEY GOT to town in time to read the evening papers. A nut named Pelley was going to be holding something called a Silver Shirt rally about a mile north of where they had to play. The SPHAs sensed a setup. It was like tiptoeing into a furnace.

The local JCC had a dormitory. Gottlieb set them up to bunk there; he figured it'd be safer than a hotel. There were adjacent showers and a kosher restaurant next door. Plus, it was free, always a desirable characteristic for a place. He'd blown a lot of dough in Chicago. Inky and Natalya had plans to visit a hotel on their own dime once things got settled. If you get married in the middle of a tour, you pay your wife's way. That was Gottlieb's new team rule. Inky didn't argue.

The rest of the team threw their duffels onto their cots, soldiers arriving at basic training. Most of the guys hit the showers. Zinkoff went out for bagels. Litwack studied the papers. Inky lay on a cot and smoked. Natalya curled at his feet and read a book, purring. Brother Shostack messed with his violin, plucking the strings carefully, like a barnyard chicken pecking at seed.

Gottlieb sat in a chair with his head in his hands.

"Why did I do this?" he moaned. "Why? Why?"

"No use whining now, Eddie," Inky said. "We're here."

"Is that supposed to make me feel better?"

"I don't care how you feel."

"You're a sweetheart," Gottlieb said. "I should have known it was going to be more than a basketball game. I should have known they'd have an army."

"That's exaggerating," Inky said. "They won't have an army."

"Will they have more than ten?"

"You can count on that."

"Then it's an army."

"Would you mugs relax?" Litwack said. "I know a guy."

"Whaddya mean?" Gottlieb said. "We *all* know guys."

"I mean I know a guy here who might be able to help us."

"Help us how?" Gottlieb said.

"However we need him to," said Litwack.

"We need a lot. Who is this guy again?"

"Someone with some muscle. My range of acquaintance is broad."

Of course it is, Inky thought.

"Well, we're playing tomorrow night," said Gottlieb. "So we'd better see him soon."

"I made a call when we got to town," Litwack said. "We're having dinner with him tonight."

"Who?"

"My guy."

"I mean who's having dinner with him?"

"You, me, and Inky."

"I got plans with my wife," Inky said.

"We need you for strategy, Lautman."

"It's okay, Inky," Natalya said. "You can eat with me later."

"My plans weren't to eat."

"Nor are mine," she said.

Shostack coughed uncomfortably.

This was shaping up to be a good night.

Inky and Natalya checked into their hotel a little before six. It wasn't top end but wasn't a total dump, either. The carpet threads were mostly in place, the water ran reliably hot, and the restaurant downstairs brought up steaks promptly. They ate a quick bite, mostly of each other. Natalya's skin tasted like salted marzipan. Then they got into the tub. Inky had sore muscles. That's what happens when your life is comprised entirely of basketball, sex, and fighting. It wouldn't always be like that, maybe not even two weeks in the future. But it was for now, and that was good.

They went back to bed and rolled around, and then they talked for a while. Well, mostly Natalya talked, and Inky listened. Or at least he sort of listened. More like he absorbed her voice, which was soft and passionate and never seemed to stop. He liked to hear her talk. She was still a kid and she had a lot of dreams. Inky wasn't that much older. But he'd done a lot of things. He knew that dreams were something that ended when you woke up, and he'd already been awake for a long time. The only thing that mattered was what was happening now. Even that was already gone.

"This is the hour," she said.

She liked to say things like that.

"I don't have to leave for a few minutes," Inky replied.

"I mean the hour for all of us. Jews are standing up and making a place for themselves in the world."

"Maybe. But you already know one person who got a knife stuck between his shoulder blades," Inky said. "People die in war."

"It's better to die than live in fear."

"I don't know about that. I'm alive, and I'm not afraid of anything. Except maybe bees. They sting."

"Buzz buzz," Natalya said.

"Let's see you again, baby."

She got on top of him, a half straddle, and pulled away the sheets. Her breasts were small and firm, like ripe pears. Inky wanted that juice.

There was a knock at the door.

"Goddamn it, Lautman, we're gonna be late for dinner!"

No one could kill a mood quite like Gottlieb.

Litwack had an address, and Zinkoff drove them there. It was in an alley, all brick smokestacks and delivery trucks. The air smelled like beer half brewed in river water. They stood in front of a metal door that barely came up to their chins. Inky could see his breath as he talked, little cloudy puffs.

"You take me to all the best places, Harry," Inky said.

"Anything for a newlywed," said Litwack.

"I'm fucking cold!" Gottlieb said.

"Yes, Eddie," said Litwack.

Litwack rapped twice on the door. A slot, smaller than a human face, opened. A face big enough to fill any slot appeared in it.

"Yeah?"

"It's Litwack. Here to see Berman."

"Just a second."

The slot closed, and then the door opened. The fat face was connected to a fat man, dressed in a tuxedo like a toad butler. They ducked down and through, and he escorted them into a dimly lit hallway, which led to another hallway, and then a series of doors, until they saw a laundry cart that had towels on it that read "Radisson." They'd walked a long way to the hotel district.

A hundred feet to their left was a room where a good-looking blonde dame checked coats. She was wearing a colorful sweater so thick that it must have taken a family of sharecroppers a week to pick the raw materials. Gottlieb gave her a dollar coin for no reason other than she looked good in that sweater.

"If you're gonna tip like that," Inky said, "I'm gonna grow me a pair of tits."

"Shaddup, Lautman," Gottlieb said.

The toad butler opened the door to reveal a casino, all red velvet walls and plush carpet and the sound of coins clanging and chips clacking. Minneapolis and St. Paul did okay. This is where most of the money went—into a secret back area of the Radisson. If Litwack, Gottlieb, and Inky had known the landscape better, they would have spotted the chief of police playing craps, several assistant district attorneys doubling down on roulette, and Mayor Marvin L. Kline himself at a poker table, where no one dared drive him away from the pot. Gals in slinky dresses glided around the floor, offering watered-down whiskey cocktails. Others peddled gum and mints and cigarettes that had more than tobacco in them. Inky was impressed. He didn't know Litwack had it in him. Then again, of course he did. Litwack could do anything, whenever he wanted.

Fucking Litwack.

They went up a flight of stairs that had gilded handrails. Inky was used to dealing with guys who worked out of the wrong end of a truck. Whoever ran this operation didn't play it subtle.

At the top of the stairs was a door, slightly ajar. Litwack pushed it open. Inside, a tall guy, as taut as catgut, stood behind an oak desk counting money, flanked by a slightly shorter, slightly less wiry guy and a lummox in a gray suit who had a blank, hungry look, like a dog that hasn't been fed in a while. The guy behind the desk looked up.

"Harry Litwack," he said.

"How are ya, Davey?" Litwack said.

This was Dave Berman, "Davey the Jew," boss of the Minneapolis gambling rackets. He came up through the Genovese crime family, shaking down storefronts and running distilleries during Prohibition. Then he switched to knocking over banks, which got real vulnerable after 1929. He moved to Minneapolis to run books, with his close associate Israel Alderman, who got the nickname "Ice Pick Willie" after he stuck one between Kid Capp's eyes. That bloody night cleared the stage for Berman and his men to run the town.

Berman knew how to be a good Jew. He charged his fellow tribesmen a reasonable interest rate, didn't have their limbs broken if he could help it, never worked on Saturdays, and sent flowers to his mother in Sioux City once a week. How he'd gotten to know Litwack, neither of them said, but they embraced like two guys who've done something fun, dangerous, or both together. Inky didn't bother asking, because he knew he wouldn't get an answer.

They made introductions. Berman had his brother Chickie in the room as well as Ice Pick Willie. Inky, Chickie; Chickie, Eddie; Eddie, Willie; Willie, Harry; Harry, Chickie; and so on until they ran out of handshakes. Berman motioned for them all to sit down, on plush chairs and couches. He had Chickie pour out some fingers of good-quality illegal Canadian whiskey.

"I hear you got a gambling debt to the wrong guys," he said.

"That's for sure," said Gottlieb.

"Next time, if you need sweepstakes tickets, or any funding at all, you come to me."

"Now that I know…"

"Mostly, we need support," Litwack said. "The Bund is trying to walk us into a trap, and we want to spring it back on them."

"You hear about the Silver Shirt rally tomorrow?" Berman said.

"It was in the papers," said Litwack.

"That Pelley character is a twopenny hooker, and we're gonna show him the door," said Davey the Jew. "This is the same bullshit that drove my grandparents out of Odessa. We've come too far."

"Agreed," Litwack said.

"So what's the plan?" Gottlieb said.

"No plan for you," Berman said. "Have your practice. Play your game. Fuck your women. We'll take care of the rest."

"How?"

"I'll show you how," said Ice Pick Willie.

Willie went over to where Gottlieb was sitting on the couch and pulled a pillow out from behind him. Gottlieb squeaked like a frightened piglet. Willie held the pillow in one hand and produced an ice pick in the other. This he stuck in the top of the pillow and drew it downward. He did it real slow, and it made a sickly tearing sound. The pillow tore top to bottom. Ice Pick Willie threw the pillow down on the ground, dropped to his knees, and gave it three more quick stabs. *If the Jewish racket had been like this in Philly,* Inky thought, *then I never would have had to work for the Bund in the first place.*

"It'll be like that," said Berman. "But more."

"I wouldn't mind a piece," said Inky.

"Tough guy," said Berman.

"I've had my fun," Inky said.

"Fair enough. Do what you do and maybe there'll still be something left when the game's over."

Ice Pick Willie had bent over, growling, and was starting to tear at the stuffing with his teeth.

"I'm glad he's on our side," Gottlieb said.

"Who wants steaks?" Berman asked.

• twenty-five •

THE MINNEAPOLIS Auditorium was as bright and spacious as a sixteen-year-old farm girl's dreams of Hollywood. The SPHAs had never played in a venue so vast. Gottlieb, in his player-coach days, had done a few games at Madison Square Garden, but that was a dank dog-eat-dog cave compared with this joint. There must have been ten thousand seats around the court. They went three sections high, up to the fresh WPA frescoes that rimmed the wall beneath the ceiling, depicting a workers' paradise where every American man nobly pumps the smelter and has red cheeks and strong muscles from hay-baling season. Inky knew differently. Liquid metal burns, hay hides worms, and most people's cheeks go red from too much rotgut.

The room definitely had rococo style, though, from the forty-foot chandelier to the shiny hardwood below. Behind the north hoop, twenty or so rows of seats sloped to the base of a stage with velvet curtains, which looked like they might part to reveal

Caruso. That had actually happened before, though not during basketball. Tonight's game would have more paying customers.

The local Jews greeted the SPHAs like conquering stallions. Everyone knew that Pelley had come to town meaning business, and the SPHAs were their de facto proxy warriors. Outside the dressing room, people sought autographs and other, more tangible souvenirs. Inside, there was fresh-baked bread and fruit. But even the subtle pleasures of a good spread couldn't calm the SPHAs' nerves. They felt like a battalion ordered to sink into a muddy foxhole for a long night.

Two hours before game time, they went onto the court for warm-ups, still cowed by the dimensions. Someone could fly an airplane in that space. They had to put that aside and just shoot and dribble and get their bodies loose. You could build a court on top of the Matterhorn and the players would still have to put the ball into the hoop once the game started.

It got worse when the other team came out. They had the word *Aryans* written in black letters, all capitals, on their burgundy jerseys, as though they were advertising racial superiority on a billboard. All of them wore the same haircut, close cut on the sides, slightly longer but still flat on the top, clean shaven, and blond. Their skin was as pale as springtime beer.

Ordinarily, this wouldn't have bothered the SPHAs much. They'd played against non-Jews before, and often. In fact, they'd massacred a team of Quaker farm boys just two nights earlier in Eau Claire. But these fellows were *huge*. As the Aryans did their shootaround and drills, it became apparent that their smallest player and point guard was around six foot four; at least two appeared to be seven feet, if not eight. A regular team car couldn't hold them all. They had arms like barge poles, legs the length of telephone poles, and hands like catchers' mitts; they looked like they'd been created in a laboratory during a lightning storm. The SPHAs had Shostack and a bunch of normal-sized guys.

"Crap," said Shostack. "I'm going to have to play tonight, aren't I?"

"Every minute," Gottlieb said. "Try not to foul too much."

Kunze's dislike of Jews was based in the vague and wrong impression that the banking industry's flaws contained some sort of racially driven conspiracy component; he also found their food and culture deeply annoying. Good days ended with beer, sausage, a pretzel, and maybe a little inferior Jewish blood on his hands. But this Pelley character took it to another planet. All day, he hosted a seemingly endless stream of acolytes. One woman fainted when Pelley touched her forehead. A man wearing a turban came by. Pelley read *his* fortune. In a corner, a young pearl in a slip of a dress played an ethereal Autoharp. Kunze began wondering if he'd sought the wrong company.

"The idea to choose silver for our shirts came to me in a vision," Pelley was saying, after talking for an hour straight without offering Kunze so much as a finger of whiskey. "Silver is a color of strength and purity. The angel—or at least I think of it as an angel—that I met in the other realm told me that silver has transdimensional capability and contains numerous little-known healing properties. It enforces our natural characteristics of racial superiority and native intelligence. I created the Silver Shirts to save America as Mussolini and his Blackshirts saved Italy, and Hitler and his Brownshirts saved Germany."

"That's interesting," said Kunze. "We gotta have a plan for tonight."

"I have all the plans we need. I make a speech. The crowd becomes frenzied. At my signal, we lead them on a march toward the Minneapolis Auditorium. We surround the building and make our presence known—loudly."

"That's not enough. What about security?"

"We'll have five hundred men. Many of them will be armed. What more security do we need? The Jews flee in shame, and if they move against us, which they foolishly might, we'll strike with overwhelming numbers."

"I've seen these guys in action," he said. "Numbers don't mean anything."

"You worry too much, Kunze. Let me read your fortune."

Pelley got out his tarot deck. Kunze knew what Pelley would tell him. And it wasn't what Pelley *should* tell him. Either way, it wasn't good.

Ice Pick Willie knew a guy who knew a guy who worked out of the first floor of a two-story office building on the outskirts of St. Paul. The sign on the door said he was an accountant, but all his filing cabinets were full of gats and saps and brass knuckles and other useful tools for busting up crowds. Business had been great during Prohibition, when everyone needed a little something extra to get their point across, but not so great since. Money was tight, and demand was down. So when Willie paid his source a visit, there was plenty of stock at the bottom of the filing cabinets.

Willie gave the guy a hundred and a cardboard box and told him to fill the box to the top. When that was done, they loaded the box onto a dolly and wheeled it out to Willie's car. Willie sapped the guy and took back his hundred.

A half hour later, he wheeled the weapon dolly into the Radisson, where Davey the Jew was presiding over a meeting of cruel-looking brutes. As soon as he'd met with the SPHAs, the call had gone out that Berman needed muscle and was willing to pay.

"Bring everything and everybody you got," he said. Locally, he'd gotten about twenty-five bites, as well as good numbers from Madison and Milwaukee, a few from Duluth, where tough Jews were in short supply, and a stone criminal who was hiding out with his extra wife in Fargo. The Chicago outfit, or at least the section of it that favored Berman, had sent up ten hard-worn men who lived without fear in their eyes. They'd survived Capone. By comparison, this would be a cupcake party.

"I see Willie's here with our supplies," Berman said.

"He gave me a discount," said Ice Pick Willie.

"As well he should have."

Berman turned to his group. You couldn't find a better collection of Jewish thugs in the Midwest. It made him almost teary with pride. He opened up the box of gats and saps and brass knuckles and clubs.

"Gentlemen," he said, "pick your poison. And then do as we discussed."

They'd discussed a lot.

It was going to be a busy night.

The game didn't sell ten thousand tickets. Crowds that large were reserved for the state high school basketball championships, what Minnesotans called "The Big Show." But it sold enough. Some circuses didn't fill this many seats in six months. They were going to throw the Jews to the lions. Or maybe the lions to the Jews.

Gottlieb gathered the SPHAs at the lockers. Fear drifted on the air like a hint of cheap cologne. There was also a hint of cheap cologne on the air because Fitch had seen a couple of candy girls he'd liked. Litwack had suited up, to be played only in an emergency. But since tonight's game looked like it was going to contain many emergencies, Litwack was probably going to play. For once, Inky admitted to himself, the team needed Litwack.

"Look," Eddie said, "we all know this is gonna be tough. But we'll just have to play our game."

"What the hell does that mean, Eddie?" said Inky. "Our game is basketball. We don't have another game to play."

"Goddammit, Lautman, don't be such a smart aleck!"

Gottlieb's voice got low and serious. His sentimental side was a horror to behold.

"Look, boys," he said, "I know I got us into this, and I know that I can't get us out of it. Only you can do that."

"We ain't takin' a dive," Inky said.

"I would never ask you to," said Gottlieb. "You're the best bas-ketball team I've ever seen, and I've seen a lot of 'em. It doesn't matter how tall the other team is, or how strong, or even how fast. What matters is how *good* they are. But no matter how good they might be, there's no way that they're going to be better than you at your best. You guys are all my sons, and I love you."

"Shut the fuck up, Eddie," Litwack said.

That broke the freeze.

They thought they were ready.

twenty-six

THE SPHAs lost the opening tip. This shouldn't have surprised anyone. The guy the Aryans had jumping center was at least four inches taller than Shostack.

The other team took the ball up court slowly. They had no one to handle the point, really; they were all height and muscle. A couple of them were clumsy. Inky swatted the ball away, swooped it up, and threw a pinpoint bounce pass downcourt to Shikey, who cruised in uncontested. The SPHAs had struck first.

Most of the crowd seemed to be on their side. A roar went up when Inky got the steal. But that didn't give Gottlieb much courage. The papers had said the Silver Shirt rally would be going on concurrently. Whatever actual threat faced the SPHAs still lurked on the streets nearby. Gottlieb popped an antacid, which wasn't going to help him much. Meanwhile, they had more pressing problems.

The Aryans quickly discovered they were tall enough to pass out of double-teams. Inky wasn't going to be able to swat the ball away every time. The other team had long arms, and they were accurate enough. The hoop was a chip shot for them. Once the ball went up, the SPHAs might as well have been kids climbing trees trying to stop it. Inky made a set shot, but they were still down 10–4 way too early. The ball came down the court, dribbled clumsily by the monsters. The Aryans parked two giants on either side of the lane. Shostack couldn't guard them both, and Fitch couldn't foul every time or he'd be out by the end of the first. Then it was 12–4 and Gottlieb had to call time.

"Harry, you ready?" he said in the huddle.

Litwack still carried a bit of a limp. He hadn't had a full warm-up in ten days. There was a wraparound bandage on his left thigh.

"I can do it," Litwack said.

"Lautman, get him the ball," Gottlieb said. "And Shostack, set a pick."

The players nodded and went back onto the court. Gothofer inbounded to Inky. Shostack put up a screen, planting his tree-stump legs hard. Inky rolled around. He found himself open for an easy fourteen-footer. But Eddie had set the play. As an Aryan lumbered over to cover Inky, he saw Litwack open in the corner. He fired a chest pass. Litwack caught it clean and put up a shot. It bricked. The rebound kicked out to Fitch, who found a space under an outreached Aryan arm and put in the ball: 12–6. A long way to go, still. Natalya blew Inky a kiss from behind the bench. That wasn't going to help much. Not if Litwack couldn't find the bucket.

By seven forty-five p.m., Minneapolis's finest civic leaders were gathered at the Elks Lodge. The Elks had decorated the hall with Nazi banners and portraits of Hitler. They'd started barring Jews from membership a decade ago. The Rotary, Kiwanis, Lions, and other civic-minded organizations followed suit. It was a point of pride for the Elks to be hosting everyone else. These men made up William Dudley Pelley's core audience, a bloated following of seething resentment and inchoate fear. They were excited to see Pelley, who spoke so well to their baser qualities. These good citizens of Minnesota wore silver shirts with cursive Ls stitched over the left breast pocket, thinking they looked more stylish than they actually were. They buzzed excitedly. If someone had moved to lead them in song in Pelley's praise, they would have burst. That's how movements are born.

A few blocks south, at the Radisson, Davey Berman gathered his army of thugs. He'd hired a convoy of Cadillacs to commemorate the occasion. They got into their cars, feeling like celebrities. The drivers passed around flasks. Berman didn't want his guys too sober for this occasion. This night called for chaos.

The Cadillacs took a slow crawl through the streets, to discourage jittery feelings in the troops. Davey the Jew didn't really have to worry. Most of his men saw this much action on an average Tuesday. They were cool and quiet and took their drinks like pros. Maybe, when the night was done, Berman thought, he could rent out the Cadillacs as Elk hearses.

Back at the lodge, as the rally hour drew near, Kunze stood near the podium, chewing his fingernails. The meeting room had one entry point and only a small exit door at the rear, which led to the interior of the lodge, a dining room, and a few offices, before finally emptying out into a back alley. Kunze told Pelley that they should have focused their efforts on the basketball game and held the rally another night, but Pelley, as Kunze had slowly realized, was kind of an idiot. He had scant knowledge of the enemy, insisting that a rally followed by a march would be the way to go. Kunze may have hated Jews, but he didn't spend a lot of time underestimating them. His instinct told him to move toward the exit.

His instinct was usually right.

The SPHAs were down a few buckets. They'd tried Litwack's zone, and they'd tried man-to-man. Nothing seemed to work; the other team responded well to a shifting defense. They could double-team and trap near the baseline, but that only happened every few possessions. The offense went a little better at times, but anything close to the basket got swatted away. The Aryans weren't particularly graceful, or even all that strong, but they were big, and that made all the difference.

Nothing really worked until halfway through the second quarter, when Gottlieb went small, putting Inky and Rosan in with two shooting guards, Litwack and Sundodger on the wings, and Shostack to plug any holes. Charlie was looking pretty winded; ten minutes a game was a lot for him, but Gottlieb had made good on his promise to work him hard. He sat during breaks. Other than that, he ran. He looked like a throw rug that had been doused with a hose.

Inky found Shostack open at the top of the key. Charlie drained a rare set shot. The other team missed a close one, and then Shostack was open at the free throw line. He made that too, got fouled, stood at the line panting like an overrun horse, made the free throw, and suddenly the deficit was a workable seven points, 23–16. The Aryans took a heave at the buzzer and missed.

"This ain't gonna be easy," Inky said on the way back to the lockers.

"It might not even be possible," said Litwack.

That was a rare show of weakness for Litwack. It had Inky worried. Gottlieb looked ready to keel over with panic.

A mile away, things got noisy.

· t w e n t y - s e v e n ·

PELLEY TOOK the podium at eight p.m., to tremendous applause. He raised a hand to quiet the crowd. Standing by the front door, a non-Jew who was on Berman's payroll raised his arm and brought it down in a chopping motion. A dozen car doors opened and slammed outside.

"My fellow Silver Shirts!" Pelley said. "Tonight marks the beginning of the end for all the Jew bastards in the city!"

Berman burst through the door.

"The Jew bastards are here!" he said.

His thugs roared through behind him, spreading out in the aisles. The Elks and their associates shrieked, animals in an abattoir. Every Jewish criminal from western Ontario to Chicago started swinging a sap. When the Silver Shirts fell to the floor, pleading for mercy, they got kicked in the ribs and smacked around the face. Pelley ducked behind the podium, muttering for the spirits to save him.

Kunze found himself getting charged hard by two monsters in pinstripe suits. There was a fireplace. Kunze grabbed a fire poker and started swinging. He caught one thug smack across the temple and hit the other but just grazed a rib. The thug grabbed the poker and flung it at Kunze's head. Kunze barely ducked. The poker shattered a window behind Kunze, spraying the back of his neck with glass. He felt blood on his neck and shards in his hair. Kunze bolted for the door. The thug followed.

The Silver Shirts, most of them unarmed, slapped at their assailants and shrieked like schoolkids, unable to do anything. They were old and soft and stupid. Berman's thugs were merciless, beating their victims in the face and kidneys with raw, experienced hands, enjoying every blow. The room filled with screams and moans and the sickening sound of metal hitting fat flesh. Prone bodies got picked up by their belts and thrown through windows. Pelley saw an opening and climbed through. Into the night he fled, covered in scratches and sobbing for mercy.

Berman got on stage, where, fifteen minutes earlier, Pelley had stood. His suit was covered in blood. He took the microphone, speaking with a voice cold, dark, and low.

"This is a warning," he said. "Anybody who says anything against the Jews gets the same treatment. Only, next time, it'll be worse."

He fired a pistol into the air. That was his signal. His thugs stopped and turned toward the exit as quickly as they'd entered. Berman had promised each of them a hundred bucks of house money at the Radisson, plus unlimited drinks and a lady. They'd earned their keep.

Kunze's assailant, who either hadn't heard or had deliberately ignored the final gun, chased Kunze into the back of the Elks Club. Kunze overturned tables, chairs, and a shocked-looking secretary who was heading to a filing cabinet, but the thug kept coming, climbing over or busting through every obstacle.

Kunze found himself in a kitchen, cornered by the icebox. The thug reached for his sap. Kunze opened the icebox door. There sat a ham. He hucked it, hard, and caught the thug square on the jaw. It knocked the thug down. It may even have knocked him out. Kunze made sure by stomping the thug in the head. Outside, he could hear the sirens and moans. A snub pistol had squirted out of the thug's jacket. It wasn't much of a gun, but it was enough of a gun. Kunze made sure it wasn't cocked, put it in his own jacket, and slipped out the side door into the night. He'd show these weak-willed chamber of commerce fascists how to get it done.

Halftime was a lot of bedraggled head scratching. Defense, they could muddle through with quickness and hands, but if they didn't score, they didn't win. Despite his late flurry, there was no counting on Shostack for offense. He lay on a bench in the locker room, barely blinking, looking like he'd just been buried alive under a pile of bricks. They needed some sort of inside-outside game, but how? When the entire other team could block a shot at will, they didn't have a chance near the basket.

Gottlieb sat in front of the boys, in a chair, sketching on a pad. He said nothing. They said nothing. Finally, he looked up.

"We're fucked," he said.

That was the kind of leadership on which the SPHAs had come to depend.

They came out of halftime scrappy, but still laying bricks. Four possessions passed before Inky was able to make a shot. On the other end of the court, they kept pressing and swiping and kept the Aryans at bay. They were midway through the third quarter before they figured it out.

The score was 31–25, Aryans. The SPHAs were running out of options. Shostack had four fouls and he could barely stand. In a time-out, Inky came up with an idea. All five players would stand on the perimeter. They'd pass the ball around like a timid chess player who didn't want to sacrifice his pawn, but no shooting, just enough dribbling to keep the other team from a steal. At some point, they'd force the issue, and the biggest guys would have to come up from the key. Then a quick series of cuts, and they'd have wide-open shots in the lane all night. There'd be no way to stop them. It was like lighting a fire in the open mouth of a cave.

They went real small, Shostack sitting and Fitch at center. Inky directed the action from the right wing, whipping the ball around with smooth passes, making circus dribbles back and forth. The crowd moaned impatiently as Litwack did the same thing, and then Rosan ducked under the arm of his defender, only to head back. Around the perimeter the ball went, for a minute, until finally the Aryan coach was screaming from the bench, and his giants lumbered forth.

As soon as that happened, Sundodger shot toward the hoop, Inky hit him with a bounce pass at the side of the key, and the ball went in without a contest. The Aryans all stood around looking like they'd gotten hit in the head with a rock. Inky stole the inbounds pass and made an easy shot. Suddenly, it was a two-point lead for the Aryans, but you could tell the tide had turned.

The other team made just about as many shots as before. The SPHAs didn't have the weapons to chop down an entire forest. But they had enough to splinter the wood. Meanwhile, on the offensive side, the strategy kept working: long, patient delays, followed by lightning strikes. The fourth quarter turned and the game went back and forth, until finally they found themselves tied at 45 with only about thirty seconds left. Inky stole the ball and got fouled on the breakaway. He hadn't been close to shooting; they'd have to inbound the ball.

Litwack hadn't been making anything all day. He was one for seven. But, in the huddle, Gottlieb called the play for him anyway.

"Goddammit, Eddie!" Inky said. "I've got twenty points out there!"

"This isn't about you, Lautman!" Gottlieb said. "Get the ball in Litwack's hands or sit down!"

"He's right, Eddie," said Litwack. "Inky should take the shot. This is his team."

Even when he was being gracious, Litwack annoyed Inky. But he also appreciated it. He could win this thing.

Gottlieb sighed.

"The two of you are gonna kill me," he said. "Lemme see what I can do."

They left the huddle. Five sweaty warriors were ready to take down an army of Aryan giants. The SPHAs strolled down the court with confidence, swagger, and purpose. The other guys had size, but the SPHAs had everything else. Here came the fire.

Inky got the inbounds from Fitch. He dribbled left. The other team swarmed like mantises. Three of them got him in a trap, their arms like a cage. They swatted at him. He cradled the ball in his arms desperately, not letting them get a hand on it; he knew there was no way he could win a jump, and he had even less chance of getting off a shot. The clock ticked down to ten. Through their legs, he saw Litwack standing alone, calling for the ball.

Fucking Litwack.

Inky palmed the ball with his right hand, pushed off just a little with his left, and shot the ball through an open pair of Aryan bird legs. Litwack caught the ball low, lifted it to his chest, and with a smooth motion, let it go as the buzzer sounded. The ball flew high and smooth and true and went through the net without touching the rim.

Jews stormed the court, whooping. The Aryans slumped away. One of them extended a hand to Inky in congratulations, and Inky took it. He'd seen the real enemy up close, and it wasn't this guy. This guy was just another basketball player.

Gottlieb ran around in circles, throwing up papers like it was the last day of school. Litwack and Inky ran toward each other. Inky jumped into Litwack's arms.

"Nice pass, Lautman," Litwack said.

"You're a ball hog," Inky said.

Litwack put Inky down. Inky turned around and there was Natalya standing behind him. They kissed like he'd been gone for years. The air filled with music and confetti. The night belonged to the SPHAs.

Inky heard a voice from behind him.

"Lautman!" it said.

He turned. It was Kunze, hair messed and sweaty, his neck and shirtfront caked with blood. He pointed a gun at Natalya's head.

"Say good-bye to your girl," Kunze said.

Natalya screamed. Kunze cocked the pistol and fired. Inky twirled her behind him. The bullet hit flesh with a sickening splat. Inky checked his neck and his gut. No blood. Natalya collapsed to the floor. Inky started to shake.

Kunze looked around. There was no clean escape hatch, except into the crowd. He turned and ran toward the Aryan lockers. Inky followed, a couple of lengths behind. Kunze ducked down. Inky lowered his head. He saw Kunze squirting through, low, toward a side door. Then he shot upright and ditched the pistol in a trash can. Kunze lacked subtlety. He pushed open some fire doors and ran out into the night, where a stream of people enveloped him.

Inky couldn't see him. He knew where Kunze lived. If the bastard had killed Natalya, he wouldn't be alive for long.

Kunze found a cab at the curb. He still had forty bucks in his pocket, more than enough to get to the bus station and pay for his ticket out of this town. It had been a disaster, but not the ultimate disaster. At the very least, a Jew had been shot.

Getting into the cab, Kunze saw a Star of David hanging from the rearview. The driver, who had big, beefy hands and a surly expression, turned around. Not good.

"Hey, mac," the driver said. "What's with all the blood?"

"Got a little crazy in there," Kunze said.

"Davey the Jew says hello," said the cabbie as his fist moved toward Kunze's face.

Meanwhile, Inky went back into the arena. Much to his relief, he saw Natalya sitting up, unharmed. She had her brother's head in her lap and was sobbing.

"Come on, Charlie," she said.

There was a hole where Shostack's left temple used to be. Something unpleasant oozed out.

"Oh no," Inky said.

Charlie Shostack had set his last pick.

In accordance with Jewish law, they staged a "burial" for Shostack in Minneapolis forty-eight hours after he died. But the real laying to rest happened ten days later, in his family plot in the Jewish cemetery on Oxford Avenue. Nearly five hundred people attended the memorial service. Gottlieb's eulogy called Shostack a "man, musician, scholar, and the finest post player in America. We'll not soon see the likes of him again." Inky and Natalya sat in the front row, with Shostack's parents. Natalya didn't weep for her brother. She was done with tears.

Two weeks after that, Count Paul von Lilienfeld-Toal's print shop at the corner of Sixth and Wyoming burned to the ground, leaving the Philadelphia branch of the German American Bund without a headquarters. The Bund never established another, and the cops never really tried to find out who or what had caused the fire.

If they had, they might have gathered reports about a young man and a young woman, both in their early- to midtwenties, with dark hair, slight build, and medium complexions, walking quickly away from the scene of the fire after it started around eight p.m. They might have followed their trail to a series of trolleys, ending at the Girard Avenue one, and followed them to a stop in front of a nondescript bar about half a mile away from the Delaware waterfront. They might have traced them to a dingy apartment above that bar. And they could have questioned the young man and woman about the strange route they'd taken into a neighborhood that nice people rarely visited.

But they didn't.

Inky and Natalya sat at his kitchen table, bare lightbulb swinging overhead. They toasted each other and her brother's memory. Sure, they could have lived with her parents, but that would have hampered some of their favorite activities. Here they could do what they wanted, when they wanted, except when Inky had practice or a game, and no one would bother them.

It was a good place to ride out the war.

• notes on the history •

THIS IS a work of fiction. The entire Shostack family is completely fictitious, as are David Pritzker and some of the other minor characters. But other than Charlie Shostack, every one of the SPHAs was a real person, as were most of the major homegrown American fascists who act as characters in this book.

Eddie Gottlieb never incurred a gambling debt to the German American Bund, by accident or otherwise, and Inky Lautman never worked as their bagman. Though many of the events described in this book did actually take place, they did so in different forms and contexts. There was, in fact, a massive Bund rally in Madison Square Garden. It took place in 1939, not 1937, and Inky Lautman didn't attend. David Berman's henchmen did violently disrupt William Dudley Pelley's Minneapolis Silver Shirts rally, but it had nothing to do with a concurrent Jewish basketball game. The SPHAs were definitely the greatest basketball team of their era, and their rivalries with the Harlem Rens, Original Celtics, and Brooklyn Visitations, among other teams, are the stuff of American sports legend.

Now here's what "happened" to some of the actual people on whom these fictitious characters are based:

David "Davey the Jew" Berman joined the Canadian military at the outbreak of World War II in the United States. His home country wouldn't let him fight because he was a convicted felon. He fought with distinction in an armored-car reconnaissance regiment out of Manitoba. After the war, Mayor Hubert Humphrey busted up Berman's Minneapolis rackets, so he moved to Las Vegas, where he took over mob operations after the assassination of Bugsy Siegel. He died on the operating table during colon surgery in 1957.

William Dudley Pelley disbanded the Silver Shirts Legion after Pearl Harbor. In 1942, the government arrested him and charged him with high treason and sedition. He served a ten-year prison sentence and spent the rest of his life battling charges of securities fraud. He died in Indiana in 1965 and was buried, at his request, in an unmarked grave.

Fritz Julius Kuhn was indicted in 1939 on charges of having embezzled more than $15,000 from the German American Bund. After several years in Sing Sing, he was sent to an internment camp in Texas and was subsequently deported to Germany, where he faced charges during the country's postwar "denazification." He died near Munich, a broken man, in 1951.

Gerhard Wilhelm Kunze assumed control of the Bund after Kuhn's indictment, but fled to Mexico after Pearl Harbor, with plans to escape to Germany via submarine. He was arrested by

US authorities in 1942, in a tiny fishing village six miles south of Veracruz. After being convicted in various trials of sedition, espionage, and draft dodging, he was sentenced to fifteen years in prison without the possibility of parole.

Harry Litwack was the head basketball coach at Temple University from 1947 to 1973, leading the team to numerous NCAA appearances and one NIT Championship. He died in 1999, at the age of ninety-one.

Eddie Gottlieb died in 1979 after one of the most storied careers in the history of professional basketball. When the NBA started in 1946, Gottlieb was the coach and general manager of the Philadelphia Warriors. He later bought the team, drafted Wilt Chamberlain, and arranged for it to move to San Francisco. An integral member of the NBA's Rules Committee, he was also in charge of making its schedule until a year before his death. In addition, he managed the overseas travel schedule of the Harlem Globetrotters. He was elected to the NBA Hall of Fame in 1972. The Rookie of the Year trophy bears his name.

Inky Lautman played for the SPHAs until 1946. He died in anonymity sometime in the mid-1980s, but his legacy lives on. His career started when he was fifteen years old. To this day, he's still the youngest person ever to have played professional basketball in the United States.

· acknowledgments ·

THE IDEA for *Jewball* germinated at Reboot, a secret camp for Jewish intellectuals held every year in the mountains of Utah. In particular, it came from conversations I had with other Jewish types in the fancy Reboot *schvitz*. I'm particularly indebted to Professor Eddy Portnoy, who kept me on the track, and to Ari Sclar, who provided needed scholarly insight. Thanks are also due to Ed Vandenberg, Roger Bennett, and Adam Dorn, and I'm sure there were other people in the *schvitz* as well, but I couldn't see them through all the steam.

Many thanks to my agent, Daniel Greenberg, for all his support during the many years I worked on this project, and especially for his hard work once I made the initial decision to publish the novel myself. Also thanks to Elizabeth Fisher, Miek Coccia, Monika Verma, and the rest of the team at the Levine Greenberg agency.

Thanks to Tom Fassbender for agreeing to edit the first edition of this book, to Judit Bodnar for her precise copyediting, and to Dan Shepelavy for the cover art. Intense thanks are due, as always, to my wife, Regina Allen, and my son, Elijah, for their support, and to my parents, Bernard and Susan Pollack. I'm also very grateful to Jerod and Joanne Gunsberg, to whom this book is dedicated, for their continued enthusiasm, to my dear friends Jane Lerner and Ben Brown, and to Shawn Simon for sticking with me through some tough years in Hollywood. Joni Rodgers and the League of Extraordinary Authors provided some surprising support late in the game. I owe many thanks to those in the vibrant world of self-publishing who championed this book and made me part of their family.

But now that *Jewball* is the property of Amazon Publishing, I'm very grateful to Jeffrey Belle for believing in my work and sticking with this somewhat controversial title, to Courtney Miller for her support, and to the entire Amazon team. Onward!

Most of all, I'm eternally grateful to all the readers who saw fit to purchase, read, and hopefully enjoy this book. *Jewball* has been a true labor of love, almost a labor of fantasy, and I hope it gives you even a small amount of the pleasure it's given me. *Namaste*.

Neal Pollack
February 2012

• about the author •

Photograph by Laura Sartoris, 2011

Neal Pollack is the author of the cult classic *The Neal Pollack Anthology of American Literature*, the novel *Never Mind the Pollacks*, and the memoirs *Alternadad* and *Stretch: The Unlikely Making of a Yoga Dude*. A graduate of Northwestern University's Medill School of Journalism, he is a frequent contributor to the *New York Times*, *Slate*, *Salon*, *GQ*, *Vanity Fair*, and *Maxim*. He lives with his wife and son in Austin, Texas.

14842363R00122

Made in the USA
Charleston, SC
04 October 2012